Haunting in Old Tailem

JANICE TREMAYNE

A catalogue record for this work is available from the National Library of Australia

DEDICATION

I dedicate this book to my partner for their incredible patience—to be a good writer you need time to yourself to achieve your literary objectives. Thank you so much.

.

Contents

ACKNOWLEDGMENTS

Writing a novel about ghosts and the supernatural is one of the most significant projects I have ever committed to completing. It was different from the genre that I had written before.

I want to acknowledge my partner for their patience and tolerance for the many hours I spent in coffee shops writing my first draft.

I want to thank my award-winning cover designer, Momir Borocki, for designing a stunning visual cover. A book cannot reach its full potential without a great editor, and I am grateful to Kristin Campbell for polishing up my work.

Although I am the author of this book, I am not a singular entity. I recognize that it was the kindness of the people around me who motivated me to complete it.

PROLOGUE

The flower is a wonder of life's beauty and splendor. It is a gift from God and a symbol of His creation, representing so many things. The sepal of the flower carries a heavy burden: one task and purpose—to protect the seeds of the flower from dying so they can reproduce again. The flower will continue to grow, although for a short while, until it has announced its presence to the earth, and then dies gracefully.

The Order of the Sepaline comes with the same purpose.

Ordained through their love of Christ and his spirit, the priests enter the order knowing they live only to die for their faith. Their only mission in life is to protect the purity of the holy light from Armon, the angels of darkness.

The symbol of the Sepaline represents their faith, but it also carries a spiritual presence and a personification of power. It is a safeguard against the advances of dark angels through the passage of light.

They are the keepers of the holy light of Jerusalem.

A bronze haze immersed in filtered light, and an extinguished candle wick swayed gently across the full room. It could have been the shadow of a hand from a mystic shaman reaching against the backdrop of a dirty wall covered in splatters of dead insects and vermin. Cracked miniature terracotta pots containing aromatic herbs and flowers used as incense lay balancing awkwardly on the edge of the window, absorbing any impurity that the stale air had to offer. Only a slight draught or breath of air would be enough to displace the pots and shatter them into falling remnants. But, for some unknown miracle, they never swayed or dislodged from their place, despite their careless positioning.

Next to the pots was the burner and chain used to light up the incense and purify the room. It was still smoking from previous worship, and if you bent over the shouldering lamp, you could smell the aroma made from powders and herbs.

Underneath the window ledge was a rotting table that barely had enough strength to carry the weight of a small jar of rose water and olive oil. It was so fragile that any slightest addition of pressure would poise it for collapse. It was a minimalist lifestyle, simplistic with few possessions.

It was the standard way of life for a monk of the Order of the Sepaline. They mirrored the actual teachings of Jesus Christ and followed in his footsteps as they gained inspiration and faith. As tough as their lives seemed to others, for the Sepaline, it meant touching the hand of Christ, covered by the warmth of his breath. Their mission was to carry on his work as the protectorate of the holy light. They were the sentinels of Christ.

Monk Arsenios was not as energetic and brash as the younger members of the order; however, his wisdom and spiritual connection with Jesus Christ were never questioned. Every morning, he would rise at dawn and pray in a trance for two hours. His half-torn robe and shabby sandals were meaningless earthly possessions of no value as he went about his prayers, devoid of such materialistic needs. Kneeling next to his makeshift bed with an ornate, hand-carved silver cross hanging clumsily on his bedside table, he went about his ritual of prayers and hymns. His hands placed above his forehead and eyes closed, he whispered in deep thought, "Kyrie Eleison, Kyrie Eleison."

It was not uncommon for a tear to be shed while in

his trance-like state. Monk Arsenios was said to be departed from our world and connected to a spiritual presence during prayer. A pale face and stoic, peaceful demeanor greeted those who witnessed his return from his place of spirituality. In his awakening, you were subdued by a feeling of overjoy, love, and peacefulness. It was a perfect calmness, as though the room had been cleaned of negative or impounding thoughts and vagaries of prayer.

Held tightly in both hands were light-brown amethyst trinity beads with a silver cross depicting the crucifixion of Jesus Christ attached. Around his long, slender neck was a black diamond pendant with a white-gold floral border. Often, the necklace would catch in his long, black hair and beard, pulling on them, as though it had a mind of its own. Perhaps it was a sign or the presence of a spirit that would comfort him.

The necklace was shaped like a floral sepal on six sides, joined at the tips to form a vivid image of unity and faith. It belonged to the Order of the Sepaline. For hundreds of years, this secret society of monks were the only ones who could embody the symbol of the Sepaline.

The spirit of the stone had been passed down from Mary Magdalene, and by carrying it came the glory of exercising its power of faith that was transcended only to a selected few through the generations. Only the most enlightened and spiritual of all the monks would inherit this burden of pain and euphoria, combined in a release of emotion beyond immortality—a force of extreme and unimaginable strength passed down in a covenant between the Order of the Sepaline and Christ.

A circular-designed jewel, laden with pure white gold, it contained a rare black diamond in the center, otherwise known as *carbonados*. It was not pure black as one would presume, though, but a black-colored effect that was dispersed from within the stone. Nobody knew who had made the jewel or where the black diamond had come from, considering it was not a mineral native to that part of the world.

Rising out of the black diamond centerpiece were six sepals of a flower in ornate white gold. Each sepal separately symbolized the unity and faith of the Order of the Sepaline in prayer. It was no ordinary pendant, and mystics believed it contained the power of intervention, only available to the one selected.

It was a beautiful piece of craftsmanship, a spiritual object that emanated peacefulness to the point that many in the Orthodox Church refused to accept its sovereignty or commit to its purpose.

Coveted were six secret prayers that had never been written, only passed down from the holiest of the order. It was forbidden to write the prayers or document them, as they contained the most sacred words of Jesus Christ, yielding immense power and authority over the fight against evil. So powerful were these words that they could only be recited by the holiest of the order.

During intense prayer, from the darkness of the black stone, came a softening array of pure white pulses of gentle glitter emerging into the ambient, softening light. At its most potent, the emitting rays would become strobe light patterns, spinning in intensity. However, no noise, only silence. It was neither blinding nor a distraction to the eye. Instead, it was an invitation to experience the warmth and harmony of being a part of God's Kingdom.

Once a monk was granted the symbol of the Order of the Sepaline, it could never be redeemed by human intervention, and it stayed with them until death. It belonged to the divinity of the Lord Jesus Christ, and only he had the power to grant it and redeem it.

Monk Arsenios came from a line of holy Greek Orthodox priests whose purpose was to lead the Order of the Sepaline in their spiritual quests. They were custodians of the sacred light manifested at the Holy Sepulcher in Jerusalem. Guardians of the festal greet on Holy Saturday, Christos Aneste! *Christ has risen!* They were the intermediaries with angels from heaven that ignited the holy light every year in the sacred tomb of the Holy Sepulcher.

Like the crusaders in their quest for the Holy Grail, the Order of the Sepaline had accepted their responsibility to their death as the protectorates of the holy light. Nothing could come between them and the covenant; no dismissal or intervention would deter them from their quest and faith.

There were three sharp taps on the fragile timber door and hurried knocks, a signal that it was urgent. They were followed with a slight pause to see if there was a response. However, as Monk Kostas became more anxious, he tried again with more intensity. Unaware that Monk Arsenios was in sincere prayer, he knocked a third time before ceasing altogether.

Would it upset him if I knock again? he thought.

After several attempts, Monk Kostas turned the mortise lock and gently pushed the door slightly ajar, managing to get a peek of Monk Arsenios praying.

Thank God I didn't knock a fourth time, he thought.

"Dear Brother Arsenios, I must interrupt your prayer to bring you important news," he said.

There was no response as he continued opening the door almost halfway. He would repeat his interruption once more, raising his voice gently as to not interfere with the calmness.

He could smell the incense and failed to understand the significance before entering the room. The mixture of perfume used by Monk Arsenios was only used in meditation and was customary amongst the holiest of the order.

Monk Arsenios did not respond, and his silence felt like an eternity.

Finally, he stepped up from his kneeling position and, while holding the Sepaline pendant in his right hand, he adjusted his robe by caressing it downward with the palm of his hand.

"Yes, Brother Kostas." He took small steps, shuffling toward Kostas. "This better be important."

"I have a letter for Your Holiness from Niketas at the Imperial Court of Constantine VII," Kostas stuttered slightly from nerves and lack of composure. "It's the second letter in a matter of weeks, and he is demanding a response this time in writing to his attaché in Jerusalem."

"I must say it's not unexpected. Read it to me." Monk Arsenios was not flustered or affected by this imposition by the head of state. The Sepaline Order believed in their destiny and purpose and did not like taking orders from those in authority—any ruler, government attaché, or aristocrat.

Monk Kostas opened the white envelope containing the red seal of the Imperial Court of Constantine VII. He unfolded the envelope gingerly, careful not to crease or mark it with his fingertips. Then he took a deep breath and, breathing out through his nose, he commenced reading the message.

> *"The Amir demands the outright termination of all future celebrations on Great Saturday by your holy order. In performing your celebrated miracle with magic articles, you have filled all of Syria with the religion of the Christians, and you have all but destroyed all of our customs. I demand you respond to me in writing with such assurances to my attaché in Jerusalem by the end of this week."*

"Thank you, dear Kostas." Arsenios was not rattled or concerned by the potential impact of the letter. He walked toward Kostas with his right hand on his chest, holding the Sepaline pendant. "It does not surprise me that he feels our work is of witchcraft and wizardry and not in line with his beliefs."

"What shall we do, Your Holiness?" Kostas leaned toward him, bowing his head. "I have heard a rumor they are sending a military attaché disguised as civilians to monitor us … It's becoming unsafe."

Arsenios placed his hand on Kostas' shoulder, caressing him gently. "See this pendant, my dear Kostas? It's our covenant with the Holy Father, and we have pledged our lives as protectorates of the holy light. We must do God's work; that's why we are here."

Eyes wide open and stoic in demeanor, Kostas' chiseled chin and curling black hair made way for a slight tear in his left eye. "Forgive me, for I have also lost my strength and been succumbed by fear, but our fellow monks don't always have our ability to deal with politics, and they need reassurance."

"The Amir is not the first or the last man who has attempted to stop us from our duty to the Holy Father. You are young, Kostas, and still developing your faith, while I have given my whole life to this pursuit. No man—not even the Amir—can stop our covenant from protecting humanity from the evilest of evil. Through the ages and before me, others from the Order of the Sepaline have faced prosecution. You must stay strong."

Kostas held his hands together, holding the trinity beads. "Forgive me, Your Holiness, as I have forgotten my strength and faith … and my place."

"I was young also, my dear man, and my faith was challenged on many occasions. It is how the demon does his work—by making us insecure and questioning our ability to fulfill the rights of our covenant." Arsenios looked straight into Kostas' glowing blue eyes and, deep within them, he could see the love of God that Kostas possessed. "Always remember our task at hand—our covenant with the Holy Father, as only He guides us to enlightenment."

"Yes, Your Holiness. How could I be so naïve?" Kostas paused. "Do we need to advise others?"

"I understand," he said. "Organize a meeting at the church with all the monks at sunset. I will speak to them and assure them of our faith and our mission in life."

Kostas was relieved as his growing concern for the other monks was well represented.

Monk Arsenio, an elder statesman of the covenant, was not always connected to all the monks as well as Kostas. He was not close to the politics or pragmatic in his ways, preferring to value his time in prayer. It was a distraction from his mission, granted to him by the covenant. In many ways, Arsenios and Kostas complemented each other for their strengths and weaknesses, forming a formidable connection and partnership in faith.

1 YOU CAN'T HIDE

The church door thumped behind her, closing unexpectedly. Then an ominous breeze of icy cold air swept through the center aisle. Clarisse shivered and jolted from the impromptu echoes around her. A tingling up her spine accentuated the goosebumps on both arms.

Wearing a short-sleeve T-shirt on a cold night showed her lack of preparedness in these parts. It got cold at night, despite the warmth during the day. It made no difference in Old Tailem Town, an uninhabited, pioneering ghost town that drew in tourists passing through on the main highway.

A group of people could be heard on the steps of the church while Clarisse was locked inside the pitch black house of God, used for paranormal tours and occasional church services. The church's interior accentuated an uncanny, creepy sensation. The only light visible came from the full moon filtering through the ornamental windows, creating an illusion of yellow and green haze that seeped from the custom-made stained glass, not enough to navigate her way around. Luckily, Clarisse carried a flashlight for the tour as a standard article to see through the pitch-black town with only one streetlight.

Clarisse could not understand where the breeze originated. *Everything is shut*, she thought. Unless a window had flung open at the back of the church. It felt synonymous with a ghost spirit. Oh yes, Clarisse had felt this type of intrusion before from the dark spirit world. A message, their way of introduction in the first instance—a warning.

It was not your typical evening breeze, it carried a fouled, caustic stench that distinguished it from the natural environment. Experienced spirit hunters who connected to the dark world knew all about it, recognized it. It was what set the warning bells ringing. Something was out there.

Clarisse waved her flashlight around the room to find nothing out of the ordinary then took a step forward. Underneath her boots, an uneven surface shifted slightly from one side to the other. If she hadn't been paying attention, she would have missed it. But that was what differentiated her from the others. She could sense and feel things that most people dismissed altogether, making nothing of it.

She tapped her boots again, like a Spanish dancer, discovering a trapdoor leading underneath the church. The trapdoor was constructed to blend into the hardwood panels that formed the flooring, located in a dark place at the back of the center aisle and to one side. Not a place tourists would gravitate toward but ideally designed to be hidden from view.

There was a fast flash of light that lasted a millisecond, followed by another. There was no storm outside, no lightning, for it to have been caused by the elements.

She squinted more than once as the strength of the light momentarily blinded her, like a camera's flash. A smell of magnesium and potassium filled the air instantly, typical of the illuminations used by late eighteenth-century photographers. Clarisse shook her head as her vision returned quickly. Someone was in the room and not from this world—she sensed its presence.

There was another bright flash of light, but this time followed by a child's giggle.

She folded her arms and put her fingertips on her chin, concentrating. This was not a new sound to her. It belonged to someone who she had associated with before.

There was another giggle, accompanied by little

footsteps racing across the timber floor panels as they creaked and tapped audaciously, like a rhythmic tap dancer.

Most people would be running for the doors screaming, but not Clarisse. Although she was apprehensive, which raised her awareness and heightened her senses, she was not frightened.

"I know it's you, Little Charlie … So, you followed me here to Old Tailem Town?" Clarisse placed her hands on her hips and waited for him to react. He was still a child, merely seeking the attention of an adult.

There was another giggle but louder and more pronounced this time. He was responding in the only way he knew how.

"You don't need to stay in this transient world. I know how to release your spirit," said Clarisse.

A loud bang came from the ceiling that she could not distinguish. She thought it sounded like something had collided with the church beam, so Clarisse directed her flashlight instantly to the roof, to her horror.

Little Charlie had thrown a rope over the beam with the noose around his neck. He hung on to the beam like a monkey then jumped from it like a bungee jumper. He hung himself, gasping for air, while his legs dangled and kicked underneath him.

Clarisse watched in trepidation as the hideous image of Little Charlie played out in front of her in a gruesome display of evil. He moaned until his lungs were emptied of air, and his head tilted to the side, lifeless and devoid of any pain.

There was another flash of light and the smell of magnesium again. She blinked momentarily to maintain her focus on him, bizarre as it might seem.

He hung with the rope around his neck, his tongue sticking out of a red face starved of oxygen. At the same time, he was smiling as though he was only having fun. Death was a reenactment that he had become accustomed to, to the point he thought it funny, a way of horrifying others and making them pay attention. He had a young mind—innocent and conditioned to get the attention of others. Little Charlie didn't know whether he was dead or alive; he was far too young to understand. As far as he was concerned, tying a loop around his neck, jumping, and choking to death made him realize he felt no pain. He could do it over and over again.

Clarisse knew from her encounter in Hartley that Little Charlie was an attention seeker and someone who liked to cling on to you. That could explain how he had ended up in Old Tailem Town. Running away from evil might seem like a good idea at the time, but you could not hide.

"Come over here, Little Charlie. There is nothing to be afraid of," she said.

He replied with a cheeky grin on his boyish face. His mousy brown hair thrown from side to side, he signaled with his right index finger, waving it left to right many times.

"*Nuh-uh*," he mimed, his way of saying *no*.

Something was preventing him, holding him back from getting anywhere near Clarisse, and every time she waved him over, he refused and retreated. It unnerved him, the no-go zone of a radius of six feet from where she was standing. *What is it?*

Clarisse was Little Charlie's first contact in a long time, and he was not going to let up. He craved the attention.

Like a playful child, he got back up and onto the beam and jumped again with the noose around his neck. As the rope reached its limit, it catapulted his frail body up in the air from the pull of the rope. He was enjoying his moment and did it again and again, each time with more rigor and intensity.

He had no idea of his place and time in the world, which made Clarisse sad. She was sensitive to the plight of young children in the spirit world—alone, dark, cold, and destitute. There was no one to show them their passage out, and so they had to learn the hard way.

Some ghosts at his age lingered on for hundreds of years in a transient state before they found closure. Clarisse knew this and sensed it. Although he was a monster with demonic tendencies, she always believed he needed a medium to help him find his way out. This medium could be her, if he accepted it.

Her wishful thinking would not last.

Another bright flash of light, lasting only a millisecond but enough to blind her momentarily. The smell of magnesium and sulphate filled the air again as a gray-colored mist floated across the church hall.

She coughed a few times and covered her mouth from the pungent stench while blinking rapidly to get her vision back, only to encounter an image from hell.

A young boy with an angular face, no ears, a broken nose, and a stitched-up scar from his eye to his lip was inches from her face. It looked like he had been in a horrific accident, with his distorted body parts and bloodstained bandages holding his head together. With a pale face, dark eyes protruded from the rigid cheekbones of the evil incarnation.

Clarisse dropped her flashlight and screamed, as she could not fathom the evil, grotesque image. The ghost who stood before her was young but had been around for longer. He was more experienced, and she could sense his capacity to intimidate.

Meanwhile, Little Charlie was seated on the ceiling beam while flicking his rope like a lasso, smiling as he took in the sideshow. It was entertaining for him to watch his ghastly friend show off a few tricks on how to frighten mortal beings.

The church door flung open to the chant of an Aussie man with a distinct Australian accent—Digger.

"G'day, miss. Are you in here?" He flashed a high-intensity beam directly toward her. "Oh, there you are. I thought I heard ya screaming yer lungs out."

Clarisse looked directly toward the man who was wearing a black polo shirt with the white emblem, *Old Tailem Paranormal Tours*. It was the tour guide. She instantly recognized him, with his scruffy brown hair down to his shoulders, thick eyebrows, and a boxer's nose.

"What is the matter, luv? You look shit scared. Seen a ghost, have ya?"

Clarisse stood frozen and did not mutter a word.

"Come on; we've got to get going," said Digger.

Clarisse nodded then slowly turned to head toward the door, still unsure if she should or not. She had the image of the devil locked in her mind, flashing in a sequence of snap photography. It was the stuff of nightmares and not for the fainthearted. It had captured her intense curiosity of the spiritual world.

Whatever it was, the manifestation had gone out of its way to announce itself.

"One of the blokes in the van saw a flash of light in the church. I thought he was bonkers, that the paranormal tour was getting to him. Then I realized I was down one person on headcount. Can't leave ya behind in this joint." He pointed Clarisse with his flashlight toward the van a few feet away. "Let's get ya home. You don't want to be caught out here at night. There have been sightings of mongrel dogs in the main street, looking for food."

"What type of dog?"

"It's a scruffy Aussie dog that lives in the wild. They look harmless but are known to be vicious. A dingo."

"Like a wolf?"

"Yeah, I suppose. Similar, but not as nasty."

Clarisse took her seat in the van for the ten-minute drive back to the motel accommodation at Old Tailem Bend. She was shaken from her encounter with the evil entity but wanted to recapture the details in her mind. It was not as simple as being frightened then forgetting about it. Little Charlie had managed to find her and had somehow worked out that she would be in Old Tailem Town. But he never acted alone—too young and immature. There was something else lurking in Old Tailem Town that was pulling the strings, something more sinister, intense, and powerful. It had history behind it, knowledge, and a reputation accumulated over a long period of time, perhaps centuries. A bender, a manipulator, on a quest for supremacy, to continue with their deceit, lies, and betrayal. Whatever the entity was, it had chosen Clarisse to start a conflict. It knew about her already, and her reputation had preceded her.

As the van headed into the darkness of the main road to Old Tailem Bend, she instinctively looked back at the old Uniting Church. In the reflection of the window, she captured the outline of a ghostly figure.

Clarisse jolted slightly and felt a tingle up her spine, causing her to shiver. She shook her head and blinked slowly, thinking it was a distortion of the moonlight, a reflection.

It was the apparition of Little Charlie, grinding his teeth with that clattering sound. He clawed at the window with black, broken fingernails that left a mosaic of ominous red. Then, in one big burst, Little Charlie's face was plastered against the window next to her seat. His elongated tongue slimed all over, licking profusely while making a heinous sound. His hands suctioned on the window, like a spider, as he managed to hold on to the van while moving.

Everyone in the van turned to see what the fuss was about, as Clarisse was acting strange. They were unsure about her.

"Did you see that?" she asked.

"See what? There is nothing there, miss," said Digger, holding on to the wheel and juggling a can of soda, his eyes glued to Clarisse.

"That thing on the window … You didn't see it?"

"Nothing there, miss. Bloody kangaroos jumping around in the night, I reckon. They get blinded by car lights and lose their sense of direction."

Clarisse sat back in her seat and took a deep breath while everyone else pretended to mind their own business.

"I want to let everyone know about tomorrow," said Digger. He was looking in the rearview mirror with an audacious smile. "I'm going to throw some shrimps on the barbie around two p.m., and if you don't like the little critters, I will have some snags and a chook instead."

Everyone on the bus nodded, acknowledging his invitation.

"Oh, it's going to be warm in the arvo, so bring a slab of cold ones!"

Clarisse had trouble understanding his Australian slang but managed to work out that there was a complimentary BBQ in the afternoon, or arvo. She was not sure what he meant by a cold one, but Harry, her partner, would know.

What is Little Charlie doing in Old Tailem Town? she thought. She had left him behind in Hartley, believing never to see him again. However, there was something more menacing here—another evil entity lurking in another church, much more potent than Little Charlie.

I need to go back there tomorrow.

Her analytical mind was in overdrive, restless yet unperturbed by today's events. They presented her with a spiritual challenge, and she wanted to know more.

2 THE SHAMAN

Wolseley Methodist Church of 1900, now the Uniting Church, Old Tailem Town Village in South Australia, was constructed of corrugated iron and taken to Old Tailem Town Village in 1988.

"That smells nice, Digger. The snags are the sausages, right?" asked Clarisse. She was enjoying the afternoon barbie in the South Australian sun. The thick natural bush flora that spread amongst the gum trees created the perfect setting for an Aussie arvo of bush tucker.

"Yeah, luv, the snags are the sausages, and the shrimps are looking awesome," said Digger. He was undersized, and the tightly wrapped apron meant he could hardly breathe. He waved his tongs around in the air. "Come over, you lot, the tucker is ready."

A stream of people, comprising tourists from across the border and overseas, made their way over. The overseas tourists had difficulty with Digger's lingo, but he made up for it in his personality—the man had tons of expressions and was suited to the tourism game.

"Do you want a coldie, luv?" asked Digger.

"You mean a beer?" Clarisse couldn't understand his slang.

"Yeah, luv, good ol' South Australian beer from the local brewery up the road. Look at the frost on the glass—that's how cold it is." He grabbed his pint-sized glass, drank it down, and smiled. "Ah … the best beer in the world."

Clarisse found Digger to be a gentle type of larrikin and sympathetic.

"I wanted to ask you something … about the church in Old Tailem Town."

"Oh yeah? Shoot away, luv. What do ya wanna know?"

Clarisse hesitated for a moment while clasping her tall glass of lemon, lime, and bitters, a local Australian non alcoholic drink. "I want to know more about that church. The history, you know. It seems like there are a lot of memories tied up in that place."

"I don't often get asked questions about the church after the paranormal tour. Most people want to forget about it and leave."

Clarisse smiled and crossed her arms. "I'm into supernatural stories."

"Well, good on ya, luv. Finally someone who has come here for a history lesson rather than being spooked." Digger turned away from the others and put his hand around his mouth, whispering, "I can take you to see the shaman. He's a few miles out of town. I know him very well."

"Really?"

"Shh … shh … Keep it to yerself. He's a hermit and a recluse—doesn't like visitors—but I can use my connection to get you there. He knows every bit about that church and the graveyard."

Clarisse smiled and whispered back, "Can we go tomorrow? My Harry is working all day, and I have nothing to do."

Digger grabbed a snag from the barbie and put it on a slice of bread with heaps of sauce and onions before biting off a big chunk. A mouthful of snags did not prevent him from talking. "I need to go there tomorrow morning and drop off some stuff for him, so it works well for me."

"Well, that's a plan then. Count me in."

He pointed to an old red car that was in excellent condition for its age. It was a locally made Australian vehicle—a red 1955 FJ Holden—well maintained, with a pristine interior and fully renovated. To car enthusiasts, it would be considered a collectible, and Digger had had many offers to sell it, but he never budged on his prized possession. "You don't mind going out in that car, luv?"

"Wow, what a blast from the past, and it looks brand new, genuine."

"Renovated it myself, but I had a good start; handed down in pretty condition when I got it." He couldn't be prouder of his car and liked bragging about it. "It hums like a bird when you are driving out in the bush. The townsfolk call it Spinebill, after the local bird variety."

"Do you mind if I take a couple of photos? My Harry loves fixing old cars."

"Here are the keys. Go and have a squiz around. Oh, don't spill anything on the leather seats." Digger winked and smiled, always trying to make a joke of something.

The next day, Clarisse enjoyed the country ride out of town in the renovated FJ Holden. They went two miles north of Old Tailem Town to a desolate sandstone structure in the bush. It resembled an old building that had all the hallmarks of architecture going back one hundred years. It was how wealthier people had built their homes back then, solid bluestone or sandstone being the most popular.

On the way, Digger explained that the shaman and his ancestors went back a long time to the original descendants in the area. The shaman kept to himself and didn't venture into town much, preferring someone like Digger to drop off his supplies.

They sped up the unsurfaced driveway that led to the house that had a corrugated iron shed adjacent to the main structure. Clarisse noticed a variety of mystical objects tied to the veranda that looked Byzantine, a flashback to the days when shamans used religious artifacts to symbolize their effectiveness in dealing with dark spirits. These objects all contained the holy cross, but in a Byzantine design rather than the modern-style crucifix, most of them handcrafted, such was their attention to detail.

The last time Clarisse had seen such ornamental work was in her hometown with her grandmother, passed down over the generations. She recalled similar designs in the altar of the grandmother's home.

"I'm going to drop the supplies next to the veranda. I reckon, if you wander over to the shed, you'll find him praying and meditating," said Digger.

Clarisse hesitated, seeming nonchalant while looking into the vagaries of the surrounding bush landscape.

Eucalyptus trees and Australian natural flora lined the outskirts of the shed in a display of orange and green hues.

"He'll be right, luv. Nothing to worry 'bout. He looks meaner than he is."

Clarisse gulped, still hesitating, before managing to find the courage she needed. "Sure … I'll go to the shed and see if I can spot him." Clarisse stepped out of the car then turned around. "So, what do I call him?"

"Everyone calls him Shamy for short."

Clarisse walked toward the shed only twenty yards away and immediately sensed something … different— the smell of incense used to purify the air of evil spirits. She recalled her grandmother using the same type— frankincense and myrrh resin. Frankincense typically had a woodsy, smoky fragrance, with a slight waft of pine needles. It alerted her senses immediately with flashbacks of her grandmother purifying her home.

Within a couple of feet of the main entrance, she heard a form of meditation. It wasn't a commercial version of Gregorian chant; it was a ceremonial prayer in the ancient song without the harmonious choruses of Gregorian music. Mystique, old, and raw, she had never heard anything like it. *A Byzantine artifact, but in the middle of the Australian bush?* A rare combination of verse and not what she would have expected around these parts.

Clarisse had a sense of trepidation as she stood still, absorbing the chant—mythical, spiritual, and calming on the soul.

Without warning, the chanting stopped abruptly, followed by a flash of calming light, a form of energy that connected you to the spiritualization of the moment. The flash was not blinding and neither did it make her feel untoward. It was a flattering light that carried with it hope, belief, and a sense of supernaturalism. Only those capable enough to connect to it benefited from the experience.

Another flash of light followed, but this time with a heightened level of chanting—a higher frequency of words, more pronounced. Each burst of light brought about a greater inner calm and a sense of wanting, as close to purity that she had ever encountered. So beautiful, she became so captivated that a little tear rolled down the side of her gentle face. She felt close to God and the real universe, more than she had ever experienced before.

One more flash and a spinning light, like a glowing ball, swirling above her head, graced her. It provided comfort, purity, and essence before it faded away gently and without notice.

She stood motionless with both hands over her face

as she tried to make sense of what she had just experienced.

The shaman felt her presence as she stood outside, waiting. He came out of the shed, annoyed by her appearance on his doorstep. A recluse and a hermit, he disliked dealing with people unless he had to, except for Digger, who was a childhood friend and the only one who could show up at his property and not suffer his wrath.

"So, what are you doing, snooping around here, miss?" The shaman slammed the door, causing the old, wooden frame to rattle. Tall, with a long, grayish beard, his thinning hairline did not stop him from tying his wavy hair back in a long ponytail down to his shoulders. He looked Southern European, considering he had grown up for generations in the new country—Australia. His long, black robe resembled those worn in Eastern European orthodoxy, and he carried a large, silver, ornamental cross down his chest. He was not what she had expected of a local in a rural country town—out of place and from a different time.

"Digger told me I could see you about the church in Old Tailem Town," said Clarisse. "He brought me here."

"Yeah, I can see his car out front." He looked directly into Clarisse with dark-brown, piercing eyes that were almost black and frowned. "What are ya? A reporter, historian, or a psychic? I get a whole lot of yous coming here and wasting my time."

Clarisse tried to change the subject to calm the shaman down. "What are all those relics you have tied up on the veranda?"

"It's to keep those bastards away, miss."

"Bastards?"

"Yeah, the evil ones have taken over the town, running amok for as long as I can remember."

"I have experienced it before—a similar evil in another town," said Clarisse.

"Oh, you think I don't know of Little Charlie. I have seen his transient soul. He's not from here, you know."

Clarisse gulped, not knowing what to say. *How on Earth does he know about Little Charlie?*

"So, has he been following you around, luv, and latched on to you like a lost soul with nowhere to go? The young ones do that because they don't know their spiritual state. Too young to understand how to leave this world; caught in a no man's land of the spirit world."

"Yeah, I guess he followed me from Hartley. It's where I encountered his spirit."

"He's not your problem, miss. It is the ringleader you need to watch out for. If you think Little Charlie is bad, this guy reeks of everything sinister and evil in this place."

They both stood silent for a while, avoiding each other's stare.

Clarisse tried to break the ice by changing the topic once more. "I liked your chanting."

"It's prayer, miss, ancient prayer handed down for hundreds of years, from generation to generation." The shaman waved to Digger, who was standing by the car, enjoying a cigarette. "Taught by my father." The shaman didn't mince his words; he spoke directly, straight to the point.

Clarisse nodded and listened intensely, leaning against the wooden beam next to the entrance.

"There is something different about you—I sense it," he said before steadily moving toward Clarisse and offering his hand. "Can I hold your palm, miss?"

Clarisse felt unsure about giving her hand to the shaman, but she thought he meant no harm. Perhaps a ceremonial welcome? "Sure, I am okay with that."

His hands were soft for a man who lived in the Australian bush.

He caressed her palms in a circular motion and closed his eyes, entering a state of meditation as he turned his head slightly to the side. He hummed a few words of prayer, but Clarisse could not understand, as it was an ancient tongue no longer used today.

Clarisse could feel his energy radiate, entrapping her in his thoughts. She closed her eyes and let the hymns absorb her mind as she began to lose a sense of reality; she might have been in a different world.

Clarisse jolted as her vision preceded her, like it had done many times before. Her mind catapulted into another place, in a different dimension, yet it felt real and part of the setting.

Evening had descended, and the darkness settled in the bush behind the shed, cold and misty as the warm breath exhaled from her mouth, forming thrusts of vapors in front of her. A dark place filled with dense bushes and trees, but not a forest; they were Australian gum trees lined up against each other, with smaller shrubs nestled in-between. She could hear screaming, that of a young girl, perhaps eight years old.

"Help me! It's got me!" They were the frantic cries of a child, desperate and in need.

Clarisse instinctively glanced toward the voice, seeing she was being dragged by the scruff of her red pullover. A dark, ominous evil had taken hold of her as she kicked and swung her arms in a fight for survival. The house and shed were only twenty yards away, yet no one could hear her.

More screams of a higher pitch filled the air, like an echo chamber, as she fought back valiantly.

The demon had yellow-red eyes that beamed in the night, while the rest of it was camouflaged in the darkness. It was difficult to distinguish the outline of the evil presence, but it looked like a beast.

As the girl continued to resist by scraping her boots in the soft soil and clenching her hands on anything she could grab ahold of—a fallen branch, a log, a stone—it did not matter, only delayed the inevitable as the demon continued dragging her into the bush, leaving behind a trail in the soil of its path.

Clarisse yelled out to the girl, who was oblivious to her. She was witnessing her entrapment by a demon.

Desperate to help this beautiful child, Clarisse called out again, "Let go of her, demon. She has nothing to offer you!"

The girl's scream infiltrated every bone in her body, like an electric kettle bubbling away.

The demon had stolen the child to become a transient soul, part of the evil crew. No child in Old Tailem was safe from the cursed entity that used the area as a feeding ground for young souls. It fed on their innocence to sustain itself and prove to his master that he was worthy of its patch, to show off its evil effectiveness to gain favor in the underworld.

As Clarisse let go of the manifestation in her mind, the evil entity flashed across her face. It was the same demon she had encountered in the church in Old Tailem Town. Its trademark angular face and crooked nose with no ears distinguished it from others.

The demon embraced the macabre like a sponge, destined to grow in propensity with every bit of experience it could muster from his master. Year upon year, becoming savvier and more powerful, this was what the shaman had meant when he'd referred to the evil in the town.

"Why did you do that?" she asked.

Shamy looked at her with starry, black eyes, knowing what she had experienced. "I felt I could share that flashback with you. You're spiritually capable."

"You could've given me a warning. I mean, it was distressing watching a young girl taken away like that, for God's sake!"

"If I told you what to expect in a flashback, you may not have participated."

"Participate in what? You think I get a kick over watching girls being dragged into a forest by a demon? The same evil I encountered in the church yesterday! Hardly coincidental!" Clarisse crossed her arms and stood stoically, wanting to make the point that she did not appreciate the lack of warning.

"I have been watching that vision for fifteen years," said Shamy in a lower tone of voice, not wanting to upset Clarisse any further.

"I don't understand …"

"They never found a trace of her. They said she wandered into the bush and lost her sense of direction." Shamy looked down with watery eyes, but he did not shed a tear. "They never found her."

Feeling his pain, Clarisse paused for a moment then asked, "Why do you keep going back to the moment of her disappearance? Witnessing the pain repeatedly?"

"I can take pain; that's the least I can do to find her."

"Find her?"

"Because the demon does not expect me to go back there, he let his guard down and left clues behind when he took her away."

"What clues?"

"Things you can't see in the first flashback, miss. The more you see, the more you discover about this evil."

Clarisse sympathized with Shamy about the flashbacks. No matter how painful they were, it provided him clues about the demon.

"Why don't we go inside for an herbal tea, miss, and

I will explain?" Shamy waved to Digger, letting him know they were going inside, and he responded with a nod. They knew each other so well that they could communicate through a form of local sign language.

An altar with Byzantine artifacts—crosses, ornaments, and a statue of Christ—filled the shed. Peaceful, pure, and protected, Clarisse felt comfortable, sensing a spiritual connection.

Shamy put on the rustic-style kettle and prepared two cups of herbal fragrance tea. It had an aroma of jasmine and thyme that permeated the shed, creating a sense of calmness.

"It's local tea, miss, made by a farmer nor far from here. He only makes a certain amount each year," said Shamy.

"I can smell it from here. It's divine." Clarisse took a seat at a small table at the back of the shed and waited.

"You know, miss, I know where the evil resides and where it came from—he's not from around here."

Clarisse nodded in acknowledgement. "Tell me more?"

"When the local authorities exhumed the bodies and moved the gravestones from Payneham Town, they brought his evil to Old Tailem … unknowingly."

Clarisse took hold of the cup of tea and placed it on

the table. "You mean, the demon is not from around here?"

"That's right." Shamy took a sip of his tea then set the cup down in front of him. "He's recruiting young children and trying to create an army of evil to take over the town." He paused for a moment and took a deep breath. "Your Little Charlie has joined the evil crew."

Clarisse gulped as a tingle went up her spine. Her heart started pounding at the thought of Little Charlie. "You know of Little Charlie?"

"Oh yes, don't I know him."

"How did he get here?"

"He followed you like a magnet; laid low so you didn't notice, and when you got here, he fell into the hands of the demon, became one of his crew."

"How do you know all this?"

"I had a vision, miss. He was sitting under the gum tree with a rope around his neck. But it wasn't in Old Tailem where he suffered his fate."

"I first encountered Little Charlie in Hartley." She paused. "And you could connect with him?"

"You will be surprised what I can see."

"Is that why you keep going back there with your flashbacks? You can see things?"

"However painful it is, I will one day find enough

clues to confront the demon, find its weaknesses."

Clarisse soaked in the information. It was a lot for one day, and she had learned more than expected. She had also been able to win the confidence of the most reclusive person in the local area. Shamy did not open to people this way, and he might never again.

She thought about asking Shamy about the trapdoor in the church but decided not to say a word, thinking it might be all too much for the first visit.

Maybe for another time.

Clarisse also believed Shamy had not told her everything about the evil in Old Tailem Town. She presumed one short visit would not be enough. It would take many more to gain his confidence and unveil more about Old Tailem's dark history.

Shamy asked her to come back in a couple of days and suggested they perform another flashback.

Although she hated going back to another spiritual dimension, she wanted to help. She felt Shamy's pain.

Digger and Clarisse enjoyed their short drive back to Old Tailem Town. The vermilion FJ Holden cruised along the country road like a gazelle. The original white leather seats were as appealing as they were comfortable. They did not upholster car seats like that anymore, such was the attention to detail.

"Crikey … the old man doesn't open up to strangers as he did to you. I'm surprised he didn't crack the shits when he saw you," said Digger.

"Yeah, I didn't know what to expect, to be honest."

He had one hand on the wheel and the other holding a bottle of water. "Shamy's always agro—angry—to strangers. I warn them the visit won't be worthwhile, but they don't care. They are a funny lot and think they know him better than me."

"Oh. So, many people have tried to meet Shamy?"

"Yeah, luv, and more than once. He would get pissed off when I brought the tourists over, so I stopped doing it."

He wound down his window then popped out his head with an intense look of concentration. "The carbie doesn't sound right. Better get it checked by my mechanic, Jacko."

"I can't hear anything wrong, Digger. The engine sounds okay to me."

"I know her as a baby. I can tell when she is having a moment." Digger smiled as he wound up his window.

"So, Jacko's the town's mechanic?" asked Clarisse.

"Unqualified but can fix anything, guaranteed." He made an Aussie salute to push away a big fly from the windscreen then wound down his window again. "I don't need to pay him. Give him a slab of grog, and he's fine." Digger laughed, pushing the fly out.

Clarisse smiled. She liked his larrikin style, and his Aussie slang made her laugh. "How far is Payneham Town from here?"

"So, you're interested in that graveyard?" Digger turned toward her with a cheeky grin. An impromptu comment, as he could see what was on her mind.

"Yes, Shamy mentioned it."

"Oh, I wouldn't worry about that graveyard. The bodies exhumed were criminals and misfits from a part of the cemetery reserved for the dregs of society."

Clarisse shook her head and smiled. "How do you know that?"

"Fair dinkum—seriously—everyone around these parts knows the story of the graveyard." Digger paused, thinking about his next comment. "But no worries; I can take you to Payneham Town to check the cemetery manifest. It's about one hour's drive from here."

"Yeah, that is a plan. And hopefully, Harry can take some time off work and join us."

"I know the lady in the archives office in Payneham Town, an old friend of my family."

He patted the glove box in front of Clarisse. "Can

you hand me my sunnies from the glove box, luv? The sun is directly in the eyes."

"Sunnies?"

"My sunglasses."

Clarisse smiled. "Oh yeah, sure." She flipped open the glove box and handed him his "sunnies."

Clarisse had intuition, and her inquiring mind had latched on to a thought. There was something about the graveyard that had to do with the evil manifestations in the town. Somehow, like most sleepy hollows, none of the residents had thought about having a closer look at the cemetery manifest. Discovering what lay buried in Old Tailem's graveyard, their histories, and the curses brought with them, exhuming bodies was always fraught with danger, as it upset the spirits. Especially those who had not transitioned to the afterlife. Lingering on and looking for a way out, perhaps being led in the wrong direction— to a darker side of existence by a maligned spirit.

She looked forward to her trip to Payneham Town and learning about the exhumed bodies, to find out more about what evil lurked in that place next to the church.

3 PAYNEHAM CEMETERY

Clarisse peeked through her curtains, listening to the commotion outside. Digger was leaning against the door of his car while holding a lit cigarette in his hand. An older woman stood next to him, waving her hands around very animatedly. She was loud and didn't seem to care, her voice resonating throughout the motel. Clarisse had heard her name mentioned more than once.

"You told me they were going to shoot through today, and now I find out you're taking them to Payneham for a cemetery tour?" said the woman.

"I've taken people on cemetery tours before, and it never bothered you; why now?"

"Don't you get it, Digger? She's asking lots of questions about the church, the graveyard … even about Shamy."

"I wouldn't worry about Shamy. He's taken a liking to her, spiritually." He took a puff of his cigarette and inhaled deeply with his lips pouted up as he exhaled the smoke. "He took her inside the shed for a tea, and they talked. Never seen that before."

"He what?"

"Yeah, bloody oath. First time I've seen him do that in ten years."

The woman went quiet, trying to understand the connection. "That's not like Shamy." She had lowered her voice.

"We're going on a cemetery tour and coming back. There's nothing to worry about, I promise ya."

"All right, then. Hopefully, they will shoot through by the end of the week, and we can go back to normal, hey? We don't want to upset the tourists with scary stories and frighten them away, do we?

Digger nodded, butting out his cigarette on the gravel below while the woman went back to the motel office. She owned the motel and had a vested interest in making sure the visitors were not spooked.

Digger ran the paranormal tours that attracted tourists to the pioneering village. He didn't mind people shaking from fear during his paranormal tours, as it was good for business.

Clarisse decided to sit in the passenger seat next to

Digger while Harry elected to spread out in the back, wanting the room to store his equipment. Harry was connecting the town to a mobile tower and providing internet services. The project would run a couple of weeks until Harry completed the phone infrastructure.

"That lady you were talking to from the motel this morning is very loud. Is she always like that?" asked Clarisse.

"Oh, that's Kezza. She gets animated over the smallest of things."

Digger turned to Harry and Clarisse, handing them a bottle of water. "Here, it's going to be warm today, and there is no air conditioning in this car. Oh, and by the way, if a local comes up to you both and wants to know what we were doing in Payneham, smile and say nothing. It's none of their business."

Harry and Clarisse nodded.

"And something else; don't ask too many questions around here. The people can be sensitive to small things. We are out in the bush and different than city folks."

"Fair dinkum?" asked Harry.

"Yeah, dead set. Most of them have been here for generations, like Kezza."

Clarisse thought best not to say anything, although she disagreed with him about exercising her freedom of speech. She didn't want to be that insular and gagged.

"So, we are stopping by Old Tailem Town on the way?" asked Clarisse.

"Yeah, I'll be quick. I need to grab some papers from the church—a diagram of the graveyard layout. It might help us when we get to woop woop."

"When we get to Payneham?"

"Yes, luv." He glanced sideways to get Clarisse's attention. "You wouldn't believe they got into such detail when they relocated the graves."

He rolled down his window and ducked his head. "Jacko did a great job on the carbie. She's purring like a cat now."

"I don't know … I mean, I can't tell the difference," said Clarisse.

"You gotta have a trained ear for this type of stuff. Jacko said he could hear something, too." Digger broke out into nervous laughter. "He does his best work when he's on the grog; hears all sorts of things in the engine, I reckon."

"Is that where the slab of beer helps?" asked Harry. He had been sitting quietly in the back and had decided to give his two pennies worth.

"I almost forgot you were in the back, mate—so quiet."

"I'm enjoying the ride in your car. Ever thought of using this car for weddings?"

"Yeah, I get many requests. If the price is right, sure, I don't mind using it for weddings at the church occasionally."

Clarisse smiled, pointing toward the church in Old Tailem. "Might go for a quick look around the graveyard while you get your diagram, if that's okay?"

"No worries, luv. Don't get lost amongst the departed ones." Digger chuckled. He always had a corny sense of humor, typical of his larrikin style.

Harry decided to stay behind and check out the car in more detail, while Digger opened the bonnet so that he could inspect the rework completed to the modified engine. He was immensely proud of the Spinebill.

Clarisse walked over to the graveyard that adjoined the church grounds. A lot of thought had gone into coordinating the layout, as the gravestones had been carefully laid next to each other geometrically. A couple of the larger headstones hugged the entrance to the graveyard like out-of-place monoliths.

I wonder if these guys were the most important ones back then, she thought.

She counted close to twenty gravestones, including a few that were unmarked. The graveyard could have been better maintained. It had overgrown grass, no flowers, and a broken fence line was leaning to one side from the road. One grave looked as though it had been smashed with a hammer and left crumbling. Not a good look for the tourists. However, the townsfolk suffered from the small-town mentality, whereas the cooperatives who controlled the pioneering village were starting to learn about entrepreneurship and tourism.

I might mention it to Digger about clearing up the graveyard, make it respectable, she thought.

As Clarisse walked toward the back of the graveyard where the smaller, unmarked graves stood, she felt a niggle at her ankle. At first, she thought nothing of it, trampling on a line of weeds and crushed rocks across the uneven ground. But then she felt another niggle, this time more pronounced, like a mild scratch. She instinctively looked down, only to see a small animal race across the graveyard as it ducked and weaved through obstacles. It was too large to be a mouse and too small to be a wild cat.

She heard a flurry of steps run across the graveyard as stones flicked off the ground and crushed, dried-out weeds propelled into the air. Tiny steps that she had encountered once before—in Hartley. Was it Little Charlie?

Then another ominous sound. Children laughing

and giggling while the faint sound of a circus tune played in the background. *Da, da, da, da, da …*

She immediately turned around to find four children, each one standing next to an unmarked grave.

One girl, no more than ten years old, with a black ponytail, knee-high cotton socks, and a white frilled dress, played with her hula hoop. She swung it around in motion and with the equilibrium of an expert. She smiled at her, dark eyes with thick, black eyeliner resonating toward Clarisse.

Next to her was a young boy, no more than eight years old, playing hopscotch between two graves. His knee-length shorts, held up by suspenders, long socks, and blood-stained shirt were ragged and worn out. He looked like he had been in a terrible accident and dragged across the ground, oblivious to any pain. While playing hopscotch, he balanced three small balls in the air like a juggler—quite a trick and well coordinated.

Next to him was Little Charlie, sitting on a gravestone with his rope lassoed and legs crossed. He swung his lasso repeatedly and flung it toward an empty can as his target. He liked showing off his prowess to Clarisse, even though he couldn't say any words, throwing his hands up in the air each time he conquered his target.

Another girl, albeit younger than the first, stood behind Little Charlie on an unmarked grave. She was wearing a crimson dress with frills and brown, country-style boots. Her dress was tainted red in parts from bloodstains, and her face was white as snow. It accentuated the eyeliner around her black eyes and sculptured face. She tilted her head slightly to the side, holding a Raggedy Ann doll next to her face, as her red hair was tossed around in the slight breeze. She looked directly at Clarisse, smiling while caressing the doll.

The Raggedy Ann doll smiled one thoughtful expression, blinked its right eye two times rapidly, and then nodded before going back to its original posture.

Clarisse trembled at the sight of the doll. *Is it dead? Alive? Or is it a manifestation playing out in her mind?* She shook her head several times in disbelief, thinking it might awaken her senses. Then she momentarily glanced at the doll, fixating her view, but nothing. It did not move.

How can this be going on in broad daylight? she thought.

She turned her head in the opposite direction, toward the church window, to find Digger looking between the curtains. She glanced back toward the children to see they were all gone, just like that.

Her heart pulsing, throat dry, a cold shiver overtook her body as she grappled with the imagery of the graveyard. It had turned into a small circus playground, but the connection with the big top made absolutely no sense.

Clarisse rigidly turned toward the church again to find a boy in a clown outfit standing on a gravestone, blowing bubbles in the air and smiling. He was the one with the angular face, broken nose, and a scar that ran from the right side of his eye to his lip—the same spectral soul that she had encountered in the church two nights before.

She jolted from the unexpected encounter and goosebumps arose on her body as she gasped in disbelief. He was having fun with her, mocking her, as he blew bubbles in her direction. Each bubble, filled with blood, burst in her face like cold, gooey red slime. She spat as the sensation melted down her face like an ice-cold splash of red tomato sauce.

"Are you all right, luv? Time to leave for Payneham!" Digger called out from the entrance of the church. Oblivious to what had transpired, he could not see the ghostly figures that were reserved for her eyes only.

Dark spirits had an uncanny ability to pick and choose when they showed themselves, like flicking a light switch at random. Sometimes, her partner Harry would make fun of her and say she saw things that were not there, since the spirits had no interest in connecting with Harry—he didn't represent a challenge and was a skeptic.

Digger's impromptu call had her focusing on him, and the circus clown disappeared. Quiet descended on the graveyard, as though nothing had happened.

She gathered herself and waved in acknowledgment, shuffling her way over tumbled weeds toward the car. Any sign of the gluey bloodstain slime on her face was gone, replaced by her sweat.

She hadn't expected that type of manifestation in broad daylight. Dark spirits preferred night or places devoid of any light—dreary and cagey environments with no propensity. This evil crew went about things differently, uncharacteristically compared to other dark spirits. Not driven by the standards or expected ghastly rituals of their spirit world, they played to their own rules and were unconditioned. This made them unpredictable in terms of their manifestations. One didn't know what to expect or how the encounters would play out.

They left Old Tailem Town for the scenic one-hour drive to Payneham Town, another dotted bush settlement on the main highway to Adelaide. Payneham resisted attempts to become a ghost town, due to its gold mining industry, and managed to stay afloat and functional, not affected by the same issues suffered by Old Tailem that led to its ghost town status.

"G'day, Maria. I brought some visitors from Old Tailem to look at the cemetery records," said Digger, putting on his playful charm. "Say hello to Clarisse and Harry. They are from Sydney."

Maria nodded to them then turned her focus on Digger. "Oh, come on; haven't I got enough to do? I'm not trying to be rude, but can't ya see I'm up to my eyeballs in paperwork?" Maria was always moody, no matter her workload.

"It won't take long. All we need is the manifest of the exhumed gravesites sent to Old Tailem, then we will be on our way," said Digger.

Maria grumbled in a low tone and lowered her head as her inch-thick glasses dropped down over her nose. "All right, Digger, but make it quick. If it were someone else, I would've said no."

"Thanks, luv. And by the way, I have something for ya." He took out a box of chocolates from his custom-made bag with the Old Tailem Pioneer Village insignia.

Maria took one look at him and said, "Ya know I'm trying to lose weight, but what the heck? This time only."

Maria smiled, taking the chocolates from him. "Thanks a lot for the chocolates; they are my favorite." She stood on her tippy-toes and kissed him on the cheek. He was an absolute charmer around women.

"Before you go and get the manifest, Maria, can I ask what you know about the exhumed graves?" asked Clarisse in an impromptu manner.

"Well, my dear, the locals will tell it all happened when the circus came to town and the child performers went missing, one by one. It gave the local detective headaches for weeks until they found some of them in the bush. The strong summer heat and lack of water got to them, and they died a tragic death."

"How long ago did this happen?"

"1935. Two children went missing without a trace. They built a headstone for the innocent souls— superstition, you know—and laid them to rest before the demon made its move." Maria grabbed her keys then made her way to the vault with a *clickety-clack*, her shoes hitting the pavement military-style, sequenced and coordinated.

"Did you know all this, Digger?" Clarisse asked.

"Crikey. Not me, luv. Only the snippets from townsfolk. Did not know how much of it was true." He looked toward the wall where several black-and-white photos lined the entrance in a row.

"I can see the circus and the performers in those photos." He looked toward Clarisse with a smirk and shrugged. "First time I ever paid any attention to them."

Maria came back with the manifest, an old document professionally bound and on archival paper. She gently laid it on the dust-free glass table in front of them and asked everyone to put on their white gloves to ensure the documents did not become contaminated from the oils on their fingers.

"As you can see from the diagram, this section of the cemetery was exhumed. They were the unclaimed graves, buried by the State. These people had no relatives or proper identification," said Maria.

"They are all children, according to the personal data in the manifest," said Clarisse.

Maria carefully turned over the page. "Yeah, the average age was eight years old. Ten children altogether. They were all circus performers, except this one." Maria pointed to a record on the manifest. "A local girl, eight years old, identified as Sonia."

Clarisse put her hand on her forehead as she recalled the number of tombstones at the graveyard earlier today. "I counted around twenty or so graves today. What about the others?"

"Ah, let me see." Maria turned over another page containing a separate list of gravesites unearthed in the same location of the cemetery. "Here, they are listed."

Clarisse looked closely at a list of children from up to fifteen years of age. "This group is not from the circus?"

"No, luv. According to the chronicles from the head of the cemetery, these children came from an orphanage and psychiatric wards."

"Oh, that's horrible. You weren't aware of this, either, Digger?" asked Clarisse.

"Fair dinkum, luv, this is all news to me. Pretty sad, if you ask me, how they all ended up here."

Maria turned over another page with handwritten notes by the resident psychiatrist. "See here? Some kids were put into psychiatric wards because they had no room in the orphanage to look after them. Only because they had conditions that today we diagnose as attention deficit disorder, things that modern-day pediatricians would treat."

"They were unfortunate souls. Had they grown up today, proper diagnosis and treatment would've saved their lives," Clarisse said. She looked toward Maria and could sense her pain. They both shared sensitive feelings for young children and their welfare.

"I still don't understand why they only moved this

portion of the cemetery."

"Well, my dear, the official version is the cemetery was overflowing, and they didn't have enough funds to buy new land. Old Tailem Town was free, and the opportunity to lay them next to a vacant lot at the church their only option."

"So, what is the unofficial version?" asked Clarisse. She had a twinkle in her eye, onto something.

"The locals will tell you they were spooked by what happened with the circus performers and the missing children. They sensed evil forces had plagued the town, and removing their bodies elsewhere would rid them of darker influences." Maria looked toward Digger. "Isn't that right, Digger?"

"Dead set. Couldn't have explained it any better." He was gazing at the pictures on the wall and not paying attention.

"This might be too much to ask, but can I have a copy of the manifest for the graveyard? I don't think it's private information after all these years."

"We did make copies of this archive ... before we bound it. Stops us from having to handle the sensitive papers all the time."

"To keep it restored?" asked Clarisse.

"Yes, luv. The more you fiddle with the documents

in the open air, the quicker the ageing process. See how this manifest is starting to yellow in parts?"

Maria closed the archive folder gently then walked back to the archive room with a distinctive *clickety-clack*. She was a woman of routine and detail, sometimes almost robotic and jagged in her style.

"Here you go, luv. Here are the copies of the manifest. I even managed to find a copy of the picture on the wall of the circus performers." Maria smiled. She had taken a liking to Clarisse and her inquisitive mind, which was different from Digger's larrikin and outgoing demeanor. He was more of a showman and perfect for running the paranormal tours, a frontend man who made people feel comfortable around him.

They all said goodbye to Maria and thanked her for the information. She could not resist the temptation of a big hug and a kiss on the cheek from Digger. And as for the chocolates, he was the ultimate smoother and knew how to win her over.

As they all settled into the car, Harry decided to take the front seat this time. He wanted to get to know Digger, charmed by his charisma.

As they were about to leave, Maria rushed out the door, walking at a brisk pace and in full coordination, like a military tattoo. Holding up documents in the air, she waved them around.

"Hold on to ya horses," she yelled. "I found something you will find interesting." She walked to the car window and handed Clarisse a file containing numerous documents. "Here ya go, luv. This should keep you up at night." She puffed, struggling to regain her breath.

Clarisse thanked her and put the files on her lap.

"Did you know the circus is passing by?" asked Maria. "The current owner is the grandson of the same circus where the children disappeared in 1935."

"Good on ya, Maria, for letting us know," said Digger. "Where are they camped?"

"Near the Billabong, about ten miles out of town. You know, where the turnoff is for the national park."

"Okay, got it. I know that place really well."

"I think you know it for the wrong reason," said Maria, smiling sarcastically and blinking innocently at Digger.

Digger nodded and went red-faced.

"They don't perform here anymore; spooked after all these years." With that, Maria waved goodbye then strolled back to her office.

Digger pressed on the accelerator as a twist of gravel slid off the back tires, causing a plume of smoke behind the car. "What do you say we visit them? Are you two up to it?"

Clarisse and Harry immediately nodded.

"Okay, then. Let's go meet the grandson. I know him from my younger days. Hopefully, he will remember me."

The circus camp was parked on the outskirts of the national park. It was a short, fifteen-minute drive from Payneham. Digger didn't need directions on how to get there, knowing the location like the back of his hand. He used to fish in the Billabong with his father when he had been a child, but those days were distant memories. His father had died ten years ago. Still, he looked forward to visiting the same banks of the Billabong where he had played as a young child.

He couldn't help telling stories of his childhood spent playing by the Billabong. It made the drive pass quickly as he entertained Clarisse and Harry in his usual ocker style.

Meanwhile, Clarisse read the information about Old Tailem Town and the gravesites. The ghostly figures she had encountered appeared to fit the descriptions in the manifest.

The children of the circus had suffered a cruel

ending, and she wanted to know more. Had the residents of Payneham in 1935 been onto something sinister going on in the area? An evil entity and manifestation? Her visit to the circus would offer the ability to inquire further, to dig deeper.

She was grateful Harry was with her, as he had an analytical mind. He was able to sift through the emotional stuff and find clues that she had missed altogether. Clarisse had learned that, as a spirit hunter, you needed a dose of rationality to navigate your way through the problem. Harry offered her a skeptic's point of view, and his rational mind was an asset when encountering spiritual phenomena. She was certain Harry's analysis would unearth clues in the graveyard manifest that could link the pieces of the puzzle.

4 THE CIRCUS

On the banks of the Billabong were ten caravans, all lined up in a row. One stood out as being old, built in customary wood. How it stood the test of time and had not fallen apart was to be admired. They had made it robust, unlike caravans of today. There was no big top erected, and only a staging area for the performers to practice their routine. Unlike other circuses, this one did not have to deal with the burden of animals, as the show focused on a modern repertoire of entertainment and individual performers. Clarisse could hear the thumping of the bass in the distance, blasting away to the latest dance vibes.

Harry decided to stay behind and examine the gravesite manifest in the car—he was good at finding things that Clarisse might have overlooked. He had a talent for details, connecting the dots and coming up with plausible theories.

Clarisse and Digger walked through the dense shrub that led to the opening near the Billabong, careful not to step on any snakes baking in the sun near the rocks. In the distance, about twenty yards away, a family of kangaroos were lying around, watching their movements. Digger advised her to walk slowly and not make too much noise, as it would spook them. They had young kangaroos—joeys—next to them, and they might become protective.

As they approached the main caravan, an older woman caught their eye. She was wearing a long-fringed skirt, in bright flower patterns and seam work, and a white, ruffled, crossover blouse, with high-heeled boots. She looked like a gypsy woman.

"G'day, ma'am. Is yer boss around?" asked Digger, his voice loud, not knowing if she could hear him.

The older woman turned around and walked toward them. She had long, painted nails and a red headscarf. "You're looking for Christoff?" she asked in a slight Eastern European accent to which Clarisse had to listen carefully to detect.

"Yeah, I'm Digger. I used to know Christoff a long time ago. We were kids at the time. I used to run around with the naughty bugger, and he would get me in all sorts of trouble."

The gypsy woman laughed. "Oh yes, that's Christoff, all right. He hasn't changed much, you know." She looked toward Clarisse. "And who is this beautiful woman next to you? She is too good for you, Digger!"

"I'm Clarisse, ma'am. Here to research the history of the area and thought we could get an insight into Old Tailem Town."

"Well, you can stop calling me ma'am, for starters. I'm Giselle." She pointed toward the caravan directly in front of them. "That's where Christoff is—over there."

"Thanks, Giselle. We will wander over and see if he can speak to us."

"Oh, and those wretched towns of Old Tailem and Payneham, we don't perform there anymore. Just passing by, you know." Giselle tightened her headscarf as a stiff breeze blew in from the south unexpectedly.

"We know the circus has been passing by for nearly one hundred years, but did something bad happen around 1935?" asked Clarisse.

"I see you have done your homework, my dear." Giselle walked with a slight limp in her right leg and carried a walking stick to help support herself. "But you, Digger, should know better from your father and grandfather about the evil that lurks in Old Tailem—it's not exactly a secret. And now you have turned it into a pioneering village for tourists. Like food on a platter for those demons to feed on." Giselle looked at Digger with her sculpted black eyes. "They must be licking their lips like a lion ready to pounce."

Digger became silent. It was not like him to pass over a discussion, always wanting to join in.

"Yes, Digger, 1935 all over again, and you should've been more careful. Why do you think Old Tailem became a ghost town in the first place?" asked Giselle.

"What do mean, Giselle?" asked Clarisse.

"Can you believe Old Tailem once was a thriving, bustling little place and a connecting town, a stopover for a good night's sleep for travelers on their way to Adelaide?" Giselle stopped, focusing on Clarisse. "But I sense something good about you, young lady. Let me hold your palms—it will only take a minute."

"You're a palm reader?"

"She's more than that," said Digger, focusing on Clarisse. "It's okay, luv. She used to read my palm when I was a boy, but it looks like she has forgotten me. Great fun at the time!"

Giselle took hold of Clarisse's hand and caressed it gently. Then she placed her other hand on top and closed her eyes, mumbling words of mystique in an Eastern European tongue.

Clarisse felt faint, lightheaded, and like she was falling into a semi-conscious state. Her eyes drooped, and her head swayed in circular motions, captivated by Giselle's sensory. Digger was right; Giselle was more than a palm reader, able to transfer her thoughts onto others. A clairvoyant was capable of thought transference or telepathy. Giselle could read your dreams but also helped you understand hers.

Visions of children started projecting in front of Clarisse, a cascade of pictures in the form of a slideshow. Beautiful children, smiling, with happy demeanors and a joyfulness that kept her attached to the imagery. She noticed a young boy with curly, black hair and a round face playfully laughing. Then a girl with straight, mousey hair tied back in a red ribbon, wearing a long, white, flowery dress. She danced in circular motions, waving her hands gracefully, spinning amongst a backdrop of yellow sunflowers. Other children flashed across her mind at a higher intensity, lasting no more than a second each time. It remained uncoordinated as Giselle struggled to maintain the thought transference. She was not as young as she used to be, so she struggled to maintain a steady flow of energy as it hissed like interference on a television screen.

Then it all changed. Suddenly, a blackness followed

by a shiver of intense anxiety. Clarisse's heart rate increased, and her throat became dry as her breathing grew more labored with each inhale of the fresh, country air. There was a sinister, unexpected interruption as Giselle started moaning in a slurred manner of speech. The unedifying evil had cast its net and captured her thoughts. It was not of her time and place, and whatever its motive, it had conspicuously infiltrated the thought transference. The demon was showing off but also giving a warning.

Clarisse envisioned a child screaming while being pulled by the hair as she kicked and dug her heels into the ground to save herself. But the yellow-and-red-eyed destructive force kept striking back as a trail of survival formed over the soil. It was a kidnapping of the soul by the devil that preyed on young children—its trademark specialization.

A master of incongruence with an uncanny presence, it had black horns and a body like a dog, with calved feet and the upper torso of a human. It defiantly dragged the girl into the shrub as it shook her and tossed her aside to control her fighting spirit.

She was doomed, her mind stolen, confiscated for a more sinister pathway and life of decadence. The girl then entered the dark world of the evil crew embedded in Old

Tailem Town. Her body was never found, as the demon left no trace, knowing they would send a search party looking for her.

Giselle fell to the ground, holding her head as she tossed around, forsaken by the hijacking of her thought transference. Clarisse wobbled into the arms of Digger, whose quick reaction prevented her from falling headfirst onto broken logs next to her.

Who was this young girl, and where had she come from?

A man came rushing out of the caravan. It was Christoff, who had become aware of Giselle's plight as he watched on in the distance. Not too much happened in the circus without him knowing about it, and he made it his job to check on everyone regularly.

Perhaps being so close to Old Tailem Town made him aware of the malignant evil that lurked by, always on the lookout. Maybe his family had become superstitious from the events of almost one hundred years ago and had never let go, ingrained in their psyche and passed down through the generations. Whatever the case, Christoff already knew what had happened.

He lifted Giselle off the ground. She looked exhausted, but okay.

She looked toward Clarisse with tired eyes, barely

able to stand unattended. "You have been with the shaman, haven't you?"

"Yes, only once."

"The devil has been at war with Shamy for decades and found the pathway to me." Giselle looked concerned but brave. "It will have to try harder if it wants to spook me."

Clarisse did not know what to say, let alone understand the connection between Shamy and Giselle.

"You know Shamy?" she asked.

"Yes, my dear. I have known Shamy for a long time. We go back a long way." Giselle walked unattended, clasping her walking stick, preferring people not to fuss over her. But Christoff looked concerned that she might take another tumble and walked carefully behind.

"I knew the shaman's father, a lovely man who held that town together before he passed on the responsibility." She stopped momentarily to take a deep breath from the exhaustion. "If it weren't for Shamy, that town would've gone to those evil dogs. He is the frontline now, carrying the whole town on his shoulders." Giselle took hold of Christoff's hand to balance herself. "And the townsfolk make fun of him, calling him a hermit and all sorts of other names. Little do they know that he has been saving their souls."

While Christoff walked alongside Giselle, he noticed Digger straggling behind inconspicuously, almost shy and reserved, and not typical of him.

"Digger, my old mate?" asked Christoff.

Everyone turned back as he looked up with a smirk on his face, as if to say, *what took you so long?*

"G'day, Christoff. It's me, all right. How long has it been? Twenty years?"

"I reckon at least that, if not more." Christoff walked over to Digger and gave him a big hug and a slap on the back. "I will never forget the time you pulled my togs down in front of the audience with my little willy hanging out!"

"We were only kids, and we always got up to stupid things," said Digger, surprised that Christoff still remembered.

"It's okay, mate. I think I got you back the next day."

"Oh yeah, when you tied my shoelaces together, and I tripped over in the big top. The audience thought I was the clown performer," said Digger.

"You fell flat on your face in the mud." Christoff laughed, grabbing Digger by the shoulders. "Those were the days, mate. We had some great fun."

"Is Giselle all right? She looks a bit frail," asked Digger.

"Yeah, mate, her mind is still strong, but her body is slowly falling apart. She is very old, and I mean *very, very* old." Christoff looked toward Digger and nodded. "You know, she keeps us safe from the evil in town. We only pass by here every couple years, but we don't perform in Old Tailem anymore … or in Payneham, for that matter."

"I can't believe, after all these years, and all the times you passed by, we never caught up."

"Yeah, we lost track of each other, busy with our own lives, trying to make a living. It's not easy keeping this circus running, you know." Christoff pointed toward the caravan in front of them. "Come on; join me for coffee and some scones with jam. They were baked this morning by one of our performers. If you breathe in carefully through your nose, I reckon you could smell them from where you're standing."

Clarisse walked back to the car to fetch Harry, who was still looking over the gravesite manifest. She did not want to leave him on his own while everyone had coffee and scones with Christoff.

Meanwhile, Digger and Christoff talked about the old days. They had been great friends when they were kids. Every time the circus had come to town, Digger would run off to see him and stay with the show for a couple of days, helping wherever he could. For a boy in a small country town with little to do, Digger always had liked spending time with a good friend and making some money on the side.

As they reached the caravan, Clarisse and Harry took their seats in the open area covered by a canopy. It was the outdoor lifestyle of the bush and typical for people who lived on the move.

Christoff handed Clarisse and Harry a pot of coffee and a plate with scones with strawberry jam.

"Mmm …" said Clarisse. "I can smell the aroma, and they look delightful, country baked and fresh."

They spread jam almost one inch thick over the scone to complement the taste.

"Digger tells me you're doing historical work on Old Tailem Town, and you are interested in the graveyard next to the church," said Christoff, who had a distressed look on his face.

"Yeah … I'm particularly interested in the unearthed graves moved to Old Tailem from Payneham." Clarisse paused for a moment to choose her words carefully as she adjusted her chair and crossed her legs. "I found out from the manifest they were children … some of them from this circus."

"1935, luv, is when it all happened. I wasn't even

born, but my grandfather told me the story before he died. Very tight-lipped about it and never discussed it before his death, not even my father." Christoff took a sip of coffee then pointed to the bush in front of him. "Out there is where it all happened, amongst the shrubs and eucalyptus trees. Young circus performers went missing into the night in Old Tailem Town." Christoff sat back in his chair and took a deep breath.

"We don't need to talk about this if you're not comfortable, mate," said Digger.

"It's all right. I think I can handle it. It's been with my family all these years."

Christoff looked directly toward Clarisse. "I sense something good in ya, luv. So, let me tell you how it is."

Clarisse nodded, listening intensely.

"We don't go to Old Tailem or Payneham anymore for shows." Christoff told her the same thing she had heard repeatedly already. "My grandfather forbade it, and my father never wanted to know about those places. That's why we park near the Billabong, as far away as possible. Those towns are shrouded in evil."

"What did your grandfather say about the missing children?" asked Clarisse.

"My grandfather was a staunch Christian man, and he had a soft spot for lonely, young children with no homes. He wanted to save their souls, give them a normal life, and a trade in the circus—teach them something and give them hope."

"But something went wrong?" asked Clarisse.

"Yes, we found out that one child carried an evil entity into the circus that started to change all the young children." Christoff took a sip of tea and adjusted his posture upright, as though to make a point. "Within a couple weeks, all the children became uncontrollable, disobedient, calling out profanities. One child killed the rabbits for fun that belonged to our magician. They lacked total respect for anyone."

"It became a madhouse?" asked Digger.

"Yes. And on one particular day, they all became deranged and ran away from the circus like zombies. I don't even think they knew where they were going."

"The archives from Payneham say some of them died of dehydration," said Harry, who was holding the manifest.

"Yes, and two went missing altogether. We never found a trace. Missing persons up until this day."

"You believe the evil ended up in Old Tailem Town?" asked Clarisse.

"I rely on Giselle for that. She is my spiritual monitor and knows their locations. And yes, they are in

Old Tailem, brought there when they exhumed the graves in Payneham and transferred their evil spirits to Old Tailem."

They were interrupted by a circus performer, all dressed in skintight clothing—a trapeze artist. "They need you at the staging area, Christoff, to sign off on the new act."

"Oh, I better go. It's the new stage shows we have been working on. They want me to see it." Christoff stood up then politely excused himself before giving Digger another big hug. Still good old mates, even though they hadn't seen each other for a long time. It showed great friendships borne in childhood could last forever.

On the way back to the motel at Old Tailem Bend, Clarisse recollected the day's events repeatedly. So much information had passed hands about the evil residing in Old Tailem Town. At least now she understood that the child spirits that she had confronted at the graveyard were once real people. At the same time, it was a horrid thought that their transient souls were still caught in that place and led by an evil demon.

However, not everyone was coming clean with the town's past, so Clarisse needed to dig deeper. What present danger did it represent to the pioneer village? For over one hundred years, the town had remained silent, asleep. The evil had successfully been kicked out of Payneham in 1935. Now, as Tailem Town made its resurgence as a pioneering village, it had woken up, unintentionally, the forces of demonic possession. Their target was young children, to grow their brand of evil by strength in numbers—an evil crew.

Amid all this, Shamy was the frontline against evil. But what power did he possess and where had it come from? Her next stop had to be the shaman to unlock the secret of his power.

5 A TRAPEZE OF YOUNG SOULS

The church was empty, and the tourists had gone for the day. Clarisse had managed to tag along with Digger's paranormal tour with thirty minutes to herself before he picked her up.

An uncustomary quiet, eeriness filled the room. It was something she had felt before and had become conditioned, expecting something to happen. Although a church, it did not feel like a house of God. It lacked that sense of spirituality or connection. To sum it up: it was not a place to find solace, prayer, and fulfillment.

As a slight edginess and apprehension shrouded her thoughts, she focused on the trapdoor leading to a room underneath the church—a crypt. From the day she had arrived and had her first experience with Little Charlie, the trapdoor had been on her mind, like an obsession. A magnet calling out to her, ensuring she did not forget, waiting for her. That was how it felt every day for

Clarisse.

She walked to the back of the church, remembering its position on the right side of the aisle. Flushed perfectly into the timber flooring, unless you stomped on it, you would never find it. Many locals might have even walked over it, unbeknownst to them that something was underneath the church.

Clarisse tramped on the trapdoor a few times with her ankle-high boots. She looked down to find its faint outline, perhaps only one-eighth of an inch spacing between the timber floorboards.

She heard a faint sound of scratching coming from underneath it and held her breath to limit the noise and tried to focus.

There it is again … a tiny scratch, like fingernails sliding across the timber frame, she thought.

She hesitated to lift the trapdoor, grasping the rope next to her as a lever to lift it open.

The cry of a child sobbing then scratching dispersed in the tepid air. She immediately froze before proceeding, gathering her instinctual awareness.

Is it safe? she thought. *Better to tread carefully …*

An echo filled the church each time an ominous sound came from underneath the trapdoor. It was a tingling tone that penetrated her skin, causing goosebumps to appear up her arms. Then an alarming frequency started. It felt like a soundwave—ultrasonic—as it caused a static discharge in her long, black hair. It continued for a moment until it was substituted for giggles. She had to decide whether or not to go into the crypt like her intuition propelled her.

She pulled up the trapdoor halfway to find a set of wooden stairs leading down to a vault made of stone. A cord dangled above, and she tugged on it, lighting up the single source—a solitary light bulb for the whole room that blinked in and out like a dingy crime thriller scene. The light was barely enough to focus on anything. However, she had come prepared with her flashlight strapped to her belt, expecting it would come in handy. It was not the first time she'd had to enter awkward rooms underneath a building. Of all the three instincts, the first one—self-preservation—was her most reliable and provided the drive to move forward.

Clarisse held the wooden rail with one hand and the trapdoor with the other as she prepared to make her first step down the staircase. Feeling apprehensive, heart racing, tingles running up her arms, she persisted. Her throat dried up, and her face muscles tightened around her lips as she bit them gently. She ground her teeth a few times subconsciously as a release of tension.

The crypt was about ten feet high and supported by stone structures, like a dungeon—sturdy and built to last. In the center, an altar had been rigidly constructed with a shiny black box, no more than the size of a shoebox, sitting atop it. Next to the black box, a beautiful, silver Byzantine cross with outward spreading ends, typical of a crucifix of the time. She reflected on her visit to Shamy, having noticed similar crosses in his shed.

She felt a tug on her hand as she tried to close the trapdoor, pulling and forcing her back up the staircase. She looked toward the direction of the rope to find Little Charlie had thrown a lasso around her hand, pulling her from ten yards away. He kept tugging while Clarisse kept pulling in the opposite direction, balancing on the staircase the best way she could to avoid falling. She gripped on to the wooden handrail while dropping her flashlight that tumbled to the floor below, still reflecting light in all different shades off the stone walls.

Little Charlie continued to tug and jerk her with increasing intensity, thinking it was funny as he giggled. The more she resisted, the harder he pulled, like a tug of war. It was a game to him, and he liked it.

"Can you stop this, Little Charlie?" Clarisse looked directly into his demonic eyes, pleading with him.

He grimaced back at her and giggled again.

The tugging became so intense that her hand started to form rope marks from the pressure. She felt pain from her outstretched arms and lost her grip on the wooden rails. Clarisse tried desperately to anchor herself with her feet and resist from being dragged out of the crypt. She reverted to clasping the rope with both hands, allowing herself a better chance of fighting back as she defied the onslaught and intimidation.

She had her eyes fixed on Little Charlie and could see he enjoyed the attention. A typical boy seeking her acknowledgement, it was cause and effect playing out in front of her.

Without warning, the presence of the demon with the angular face joined in the fray by tugging on the rope, a tag team, and Clarisse knew it would now be more difficult to resist without help.

She was dragged down the church aisle as a sharp, acidic stench filled the air and the room became cold, dropping in temperature rapidly. It reminded her of the vision at Shamy's shed, the flashback—the young girl being dragged into the bush, the trademark giveaway that the same demon was at play.

As they continued tugging and dragging her down the aisle, Clarisse managed to grip on to a pew by wrapping her legs around it. It seemed to work as the rope caught between the benches, forming a knot. This angered the young demon, who snatched the line from Little Charlie, sensing they had lost their advantage.

Clarisse coughed several times from the smell of the putrid air that was intoxicating and made it hard to breathe. The scent so rancid, like rotting fish and meat combined in a vat full of excrement, that she wanted to vomit.

Little Charlie was content with looking on, observing the demon apply his evil tirade as he growled and poked his forked tongue out like a lizard.

Within an instant, something in the crypt caused the devil to cease its attack. The demon became euphoric, purple-faced, his saber-like teeth oozing saliva. Both eyes flickered with a blood-yellow stain.

In the background, other children appeared, the same ones she had encountered previously. They fitted the description from the manifest of Payneham cemetery.

A girl swung from one beam to another on the ceiling like a trapeze act, showing off her abilities with more daring and death-defying stunts. She did not have to worry about crashing to the ground, because she was already dead. No different than Little Charlie hanging himself repeatedly for attention.

A young boy juggled three balls in the air near the

altar while balancing on a unicycle as he whistled a circus tune.

The last of the evil crew, a girl who liked performing a mixture of acrobatics and body stretches to show off her flexibility, turned and twisted her torso to touch her toes from her back, flipping around one hundred and eighty degrees, an impossible feat for a mortal.

The demon growled with such a burst of strength that it lifted the pew off the ground and untangled the rope. The rope free again, they started tugging Clarisse once more, determined not to let her get away. Clarisse felt drawn back into the hands of the demon. Inch by inch, he ravished on, and only six yards out, she scrambled to latch on to anything she could.

She got pulled in closer and closer, underneath the hairy, dog-like arms of the demon, while sliding on her side. No matter what Clarisse did, it was too powerful, more potent than any evil spirit she had encountered before.

Without warning, a luminescent light filtered through the trapdoor, filling the church with a luxuriously soft, white display—penetrating, pure, clean, and bold. The demon put his arms over his eyes to shield himself, releasing the rope and stepping back reluctantly while looking away from the source.

The church became silent, as though time stood still. Whatever the light represented, it had overpowered the demon and highlighted its fragility by making it retreat. With it, the three young children and Little Charlie also left. The ball juggling on the unicycle and the trapeze act ceased, the show finished. The curtain fell on the circus of young souls.

The brilliance of the light faded into a microcosm of shadows.

Clarisse lay on her side with outstretched arms and her legs in a fetal position, trying to make sense of what had happened. The intense encounter with the demon spirit had been different: plumed in darkness, ambition, anger, and delusion with visions of greatness. This demon was no pushover, metaphysically escorted by a crew of lost souls that were eager to please. And one thing was for sure: the energy that resided in the crypt prevented the evil crew from achieving its ghastly aim. It was the last line of defense for Old Tailem Town.

Clarisse lifted herself up and adjusted her clothes. Then she retreated down the wooden stairs and into the crypt, managing to find her flashlight next to the wall in front of her.

The room felt inviting, peaceful, warm, and safe. It touched her as though someone had thrown a warm, soft blanket over her and tucked her into bed, in the arms of a loving mother who caressed her to sleep every night.

There were not many objects in the crypt to symbolize the faith. Other than the Byzantine cross, there was the black box, which was French polished and without a scratch or indentation, like new.

It was unlocked, although it had a keyhole. An oversight or unnecessary as nobody could access the crypt? Perhaps the power contained within the black box had its own self-defense, unperturbed by the threat of any evil crew, the demon, or his master. All she had to do was lift the lid and see inside to discover the source of the magnificent light manifestation.

The black box contained a *carbonados*—a circular-designed jewel, laden with pure white gold. It included a rare black diamond as the centerpiece—brilliant, round, and cut by only the steadiest of hands of a master artisan. A gold sepal outer that resembled the petal of a flower complemented the jewel. The diamond sparkled in all directions while bending light—grandiose, majestic, celestial, and divine. She felt the power of All Mighty God by her side and the spirit of angels, a radiating warmth that made her want to pray and shed a tear.

She placed her hands on the black box without touching the stone, not wanting to let go. She then closed her eyes and let her mind drift until she felt connected to the real universe, a powerful energy that the demonic force could not tolerate by its predominance, a serene, quiet place.

Made of stone and hastily put together without the refinement of a chapel, the crypt remained cleanly spirited, untouched by evil, and devoid of any encumbrance. A haven for the spiritual world prevented the evil crew from controlling it. If the crypt remained intact, the fight against the demonic forces of the town would continue to ravage, for centuries, if need be.

Clarisse realized Digger would be waiting for her outside the church to take her back to the motel at Old Tailem Bend. She closed the black box, making sure she got another look at the splendor of the *carbonados.*

While making her way up the wooden staircase and out of the crypt, she reflected on the close call with the demon's crew and whether she would be so lucky next time.

"G'day, luv. It's been a hell of a day. How about yers?" asked Digger, peering outside his side window. "Come on; jump in. I will take you back to the motel."

Clarisse smiled but did not say much, reluctant to let on to what had happened in the church, let alone her discovery of the *carbonados*.

"You can admire the church during the day, unlike the paranormal tour when you are always on the move—you miss things," she said.

"Oh yeah, I agree with you there." He took a last puff of his cigarette before throwing it onto the sandy gravel below.

Clarisse sidestepped the cigarette smoke and stepped into the passenger side.

"We were chock-a-block today with the paranormal tour. A woman went nuts unexpectedly. It was hard work!"

"What happened?"

"All seemed a bit strange, if you ask me." He pointed toward the graveyard. "It happened over there. She reckons she saw kids playing in the graveyard … but kids from the past, dressed funny and performing circus acts."

"You mean, the nineteenth century?"

"Yeah, yeah, nineteenth-century-looking kids; that's right." Digger turned on the ignition and skidded onto the main road, leaving a plume of dust behind. "But when I stepped outside the church to have a look, I couldn't see anything."

"Is she all right?"

"Well, she was shaken and asked her boyfriend to

drive her away." He looked at Clarisse and smiled. "In a way, it's good for business, because word gets around there are ghost sightings. You know what I mean?"

"Well, that's why people come on paranormal tours—so they can leave screaming," Clarisse quipped.

They both chuckled and nodded.

"You know, Digger, remember I told you I saw something in the graveyard on the way to Payneham?"

"I remember that, luv, and never made too much of it, to be honest."

"I know you're going to think I'm mad, but I saw children playing ... nineteenth-century-looking kids. They were doing all sorts of tricks, like you see in the circus—juggling, acrobatics, trapeze, that sort of thing. One child was dressed as a clown, blowing bubbles on top of a gravestone."

"Fair dinkum? It sounds a bit farfetched, if you ask me. I remember looking through the window facing the graveyard. I didn't see anything."

"Who knows? Probably the strong sunlight and time of day. I felt dehydrated and lightheaded." Clarisse adjusted herself on the passenger side as Digger carved through the bends in the road, screeching and testing his updated braking system.

"Yeah, you hear about people hallucinating in the

strong heat, and it got pretty warm. This arvo? A stinker of a day."

Digger pulled out an envelope from the glove box as he held the steering wheel with one hand. "Shamy asked me to give you this."

"Oh, there is something inside … something round." Clarisse fiddled with the envelope as she wrapped her fingers around a loose object the size of a small marble.

"Are you going to open it?"

She tore the envelope open to find a black, shiny stone. It sparkled in the sunlight, like a diamond, but it was made of something else, something mystical and inviting.

Digger glanced at the stone with one eye on the road ahead. "I think he believes you're all right. He likes you."

Clarisse glanced toward him and cringed.

"Oh, I don't mean it that way. I am referring to yer mystical abilities. You must have impressed him, because he never sends anyone a letter … not since I have known him. But he's a good sport and means well, considering he behaves like a hermit."

"Yeah, I would like to get to know him better, but I'm not sure how he would take it. Knowing he likes to be alone, I'd feel like I was intruding."

Digger slapped himself gently in the face. "Bloody

mozzies! They are everywhere today.

"I can take you to see Shamy tomorrow. Need to drop off a few things to him, so it's no bother."

"I will check with Harry tonight and see whether he's working tomorrow. But it should be okay, otherwise."

"No worries, luv. We are nearly there, around that last bend. Almost time for din-dins." Digger's stomach had rumbled more than once. "I'm busting to go to the dunny, too. Thank God we are nearly there."

Clarisse laughed, as she had heard that slang before from Harry. She knew what it meant—he had to go to the bathroom. Considering the number of empty water bottles laying in front of her, it did not come as a surprise. It had been a hot day.

Clarisse looked forward to dinner with Harry. He had been studying the manifest from Payneham cemetery and had said he found something interesting.

"You know, the only reason this motel makes any money is that there is nowhere else to stay for at least a hundred miles," said Clarisse.

Harry turned his head to find Kezza getting angry with a customer. "I don't know how that woman can run a business?" he whispered. "She has the people skills of a sewer rat."

Clarisse smiled and tried to look away, not wanting to make it obvious that they were talking about the woman, and whispered, "She complained to Digger about me snooping around the church and asking people questions. Can you believe that?"

"Fair dinkum, you're kidding me?"

"Yeah, he told me to ignore her, though. He knows how to handle the locals because he grew up here, but she would drive me mad." Clarisse took one look at the menu and balked. "There's only three choices again—steak, eggs, and chips?"

Harry nodded and sighed while tossing the menu on the table. "No point looking at it. The steak is about the only meal that is half decent."

"If there's a place guaranteed to help you lose your appetite, it's this dump of a motel." She placed the menu on the table like a poker player with a royal flush. "I can appreciate now how good it was in Hartley Town when we stayed at the Presbytery Inn."

Harry nodded, agreeing. "Well, I'm on track to shed a couple of pounds without building a sweat." Harry smirked while holding his hand across his mouth. "We are here for another week, if I can get everything working in time for opening day."

Clarisse poured herself a glass of water from a jug

then added a slice of lemon. "Are they having an opening day?"

"Haven't you seen all the pamphlets and posters around the place?"

"You know, I haven't been paying attention. I have been curious about the church and graveyard."

Harry nodded, knowing Clarisse would go sticking her nose into anything remotely associated with the paranormal. "The place is going to be full of tourists, families, and school kids soon."

"Did you say *school kids?*"

"Yes, Clarisse, school kids in the busloads. I need to get the internet working so they can have communications and point of sale machines in the stores."

"I see …"

"You look worried. Has someone pissed you off?"

"Nah, I'm just tired. Been a warm day and felt dehydrated." Clarisse lifted her head, took a deep breath, and smiled. "How did it go, studying the manifest from Payneham cemetery?"

"Hmm. Am I glad you asked, and boy did I find something interesting."

"Well, come on; tell me." Clarisse grabbed his arm with a firm grip while jostling her chair, keen to learn what Harry had found. She waited in anticipation, tapping her fingers on the table.

"Well, let me look here at my notes …" Harry toyed with her, delaying his findings.

"Come on; stop playing around." Clarisse's nerves became frayed as she pointed to the notebook, poking at it.

"Okay. This is what I found … The circus was designated as foster parents to the children. They had no fixed address. Some were orphans seeking refuge, vagabonds who had left their institutions, foster homes. Some were runaways."

"Hey, that's a handful. You mentioned running away; from what? The circus offered the kids refuge and protection." Clarisse put her hands together and leaned forward, whispering, "But protection from what?"

"Like most people around here in the bush, it's hard to find the truth," said Harry. He took out his notebook and flicked to another page. "I found a little more info …"

That did not surprise Clarisse, because if Harry was interested in something, he would extend his reach for information.

"So, what is it?"

"The owner of the circus, back in 1935, was a

religious man, and his goal in life was to protect young children from a life of destitution." Harry took out an old black-and-white photo, handing it to Clarisse. "I found this pic online."

Clarisse took the photo and held it closer to her to get a better look. Overcome by a dead silence, she momentarily froze.

"What is it? You look like a spirit blew over you," said Harry.

"That boy with the angular face and pointy nose … I have seen him," said Clarisse. A chill ran up her spine, causing a relentless shiver. She marked the boy with her index finger while Harry looked on.

"Buckley's chance, Clarisse. The photo is from 1935, and I doubt he would be walking around Old Tailem Town today."

"I mean, you're right, Harry—he's not alive *now*. But I have seen his spirit, a dark soul that seems to have embedded himself in Old Tailem." Clarisse looked directly into Harry's eyes and said, "I know what you are going to say."

Harry sat quietly. He had seen that look of intensity—her sharp eyes, dilated pupils, and thoughtfulness that penetrated right through you. It was not the first time Clarisse had mentioned spirit sightings, but he always went along with it by not trying to discount her experiences.

"Where did you see him?"

"At the graveyard, next to the church. Does he have a name?"

Harry checked his notes then correlated the details with the manifest. "Patty. Short for Patrick ... Patrick O'Brien.

"And I recognize one of the girls. The skinny one with the curly dark hair and pretty face."

"You saw her, too?"

"Yeah, performing acrobatics and flexing her body like elastic."

"Let me check," said Harry. He flicked through the manifest then cross-checked with the photo. "I think it's Lucia, but no surname; only Lucia."

Clarisse sat back in her chair and crossed her legs while she contemplated Harry's findings.

"There were four children who went missing. They were found in the bush, dead from heat exhaustion and lack of water." Harry flicked over another page then handed it to Clarisse. "It's the report from the local press at the time. It's the only credible source of commentary I could find."

"Do you mind if I hold on to this?"

"You can have the whole lot. There is not much I can do with it."

Clarisse leaned forward over the table and laid her elbows flat in front of her. "You know, I'm starting to believe there is something sinister in this town—a dark spirit and transient souls caught in the middle of nothing. Up until now, they couldn't hurt anyone—the town was empty. But now—"

"I know," interrupted Harry. "Turning the town upside down into a fairground attraction, a pioneering village." He took a sip of beer then wiped the froth off his mouth with his sleeve.

"And they will fight for every inch of turf and grow their crew of evil misfits," said Clarisse. She pointed to the picture of the circus. "That is why the circus won't come anywhere near this place—they are frightened, concerned that the evil that has overtaken Old Tailem Town will reenact similar events from 1935."

"So, you're concerned about opening day?" asked Harry.

Clarisse turned around to make sure nobody in the room was listening then whispered with her hand over her mouth, "Could you imagine what that would bring to that evil crew? Suddenly you have kids running around at will. It will become a pecking ground."

"What do you mean, Clarisse?"

"Oh, maybe I am overexaggerating, getting too emotional. Right?"

Harry did not respond, knowing Clarisse got a bit carried away with the paranormal stuff. Being bored did not help either, which he blamed himself for.

"I know we haven't spent much time together here, but I will make it up to you. I promise," said Harry.

After dinner, Clarisse sat in the courtyard while Harry got ready for an early start next morning. She could not help trying to piece all the events together, her mind racing and her thoughts running ahead of herself. She had to slow down and mind map all the paranormal phenomena from the last couple of days.

She took out her notebook with all the footnotes she had made about the manifestations during the week. She started drawing a storyboard of her encounters, scribbling notes on her laptop:

The circus that refuses to come to town.

Payneham cemetery and exhumed graves.

The mysterious disappearance of children in 1935.

The encounters with the evil crew in

Old Tailem Church.

Clarisse drew arrows like a flow map—the shaman, Digger, Giselle, Little Charlie, and the magnificent stone in the church crypt.

What is going on in Old Tailem Town?

She thought about future events, like opening day, and how to unlock the power of the *carbonados* in the crypt. One thing was for sure: the evil crew were showing their hand and becoming more visible with each encounter. As the intensity grew, the confrontations became more dangerous. It wasn't about scaring her anymore; the evil crew regarded her as a threat.

Clarisse did not have the answers, but she did have a lot of questions on how to stop the evil incarnation from taking over the town. She could only think of one person knowledgeable enough to have the answers, but would he want to get involved and share his mystical resources? There was only one way to find out, and that would depend on her next visit to Shamy. Could he unlock the secrets of Old Tailem Town and how it became an epicenter for evil in the first place?

Evil and demonic manifestations did not happen at random. They were motivated by a higher purpose. That was what drove their behavior. They yielded a plan to take over the town in a battleground for expansion and influence. Some battles fought for generations and like sleeper cells, resurfaced at the right moment.

Old Tailem was making a comeback as a pioneering town. It provided the evil crew an outlet, an opportunity to expand its wings, to infiltrate and capture young souls to build its army of followers.

Like most evil institutions, some operated as niches—not all evil was of the same persuasion. In the case of Old Tailem Town, the evil forces preyed on young children, too young to understand they were hostages to a transient world of spirits and playing out a daily ritual. To them, they were neither dead nor alive. They did not need Mummy or Daddy because they had each other.

When the evil crew came out to play, they did so altogether by strength in numbers, never alone. Led by a mighty demon who looked after his flock for his own nefarious purposes, it understood the power of numbers. On his own, he was vulnerable to the remarkable strength of the shaman, built upon centuries of mystic power and influence. The shaman's skills were hereditary and dated back to the Byzantine period. A covenant, an order, or a religious sect—who knew? It was up to Clarisse to find out.

6 LITTLE ARCHIE

Old Tailem was hosting a family day reserved for the local community. Uncharacteristically full, the pioneering village put on a display that served as a precursor—a dry run for opening day next week. It was a great way to test all the facilities and train the staff.

Digger's paranormal sessions were the most popular event, and all fully booked. Starting at sunset, they were running every hour until eleven p.m. *Guaranteed to scare your socks off!* That was his motto, and it played well into the minds of the visitors. It consisted of a tour of the church, the graveyard, and finishing up at the old police cells, lasting about forty minutes. It was a condensed version of the usual paranormal tour that Clarisse had attended.

The first session, at six p.m., was organized for people who had young children and needed to leave early. The minimum age for the paranormal tour was sixteen, and many kids waited in the playground next to the car park. They played under supervision while waiting for their parents to finish—another idea thought up by Digger. It was an empty lot converted into a mini playground for the visitors, close to a dense shrub and a line of eucalyptus trees.

"Keep an eye on Archie," said one of the mothers who was excited about the paranormal tour like a kid at a fairground attraction.

"Yes, Mum. Some of my friends from school are here, too," said a girl who was surprisingly obedient for a rebellious fourteen-year-old.

After Digger's impromptu call to begin, the parents stepped inside the church, still hearing the children in the distance—playful screams and cheers like a school playground that resonated up the main street.

After thirty minutes, the parents headed to the last section of the paranormal tour—the old police station— as the sun started to set slowly over the horizon, an orange-tinted sky making way for a starry night.

Archie sat on the swing alone and not too far from the other kids, happy to sit around and do nothing. A calm child for his age, he liked to dream and gaze in the distance, thinking about fantastical creatures and monsters with his wild imagination.

"Psst, psst," someone called to him from the shrubs a couple of yards away.

Archie looked around to see where the call came from, but there was no one there. However, he did hear the clatter of branches moving and breaking off at the ends.

"Psst, psst." The same call came again, this time a bit louder and more gregarious, intent on getting his attention. A white-gloved hand poked out of the shrub, making a swirling motion like a traffic officer giving directions. "Psst, psst. Come over here. I have something for you." It was the voice of a young teenage girl.

Archie stood up from the swing and walked slowly toward the shrub, each step bringing him closer. He was oblivious and calm, considering what was awaiting him.

The light was dim, as it had started to get dark, and the single lamppost in the playground was weak. It could hardly have helped anyone find their way around, so Archie struggled to see in front of him.

As he got closer to the shrub, in the direction of the voice, a Raggedy Ann doll ducked its head out of the bush and bounced about, trying to get his attention. It looked like an old-style doll and something his grandparents would have played with as children. It had curly red hair, blue trousers, and a big, greedy smile.

A puppet show, he thought.

Archie wanted to touch the doll. It was so lifelike that it had him mesmerized, like a spell had been cast on him. He walked another foot to get a better look, more curious.

"Psst, psst … want to play with me?" asked the Raggedy Ann. *It was alive!* Its mouth moved in a synchronized motion, but there was no ventriloquist behind it.

When Archie was at arm's length from the doll, something grabbed his ankles and started to drag him. It pierced into his skin like long nails, penetrating and scratching. He screamed and kicked as panic set in, fighting back with all his might.

"Cecilia! Cecelia! Help me! Help me!" Archie yelled toward the other children where his sister looked on in horror. He waved his hands while being dragged facedown, scraping the soil and trying to grab on to anything he could.

With one hand on each ankle, the evil beneath the shrub latched on to him with painted black fingernails on white hands that looked dead as they continued to clutch on to him and pull him.

Archie managed to grab ahold of a log with both arms curled around it, holding as tightly as he could, like his life depended on it, which it did.

Cecelia ran frantically toward Archie with her two friends chasing close behind. Ten yards, then six, then one until she dived straight for Archie's arms and latched on to him. She could feel the evil force pulling both of them in the same direction. It was a battle to save Archie's soul from the kidnapping plot of the evil crew.

"Hold on to me, Archie! Kick! Kick harder!" she yelled.

Archie was not giving up, his adrenaline unleashing furious energy, the likes of which he had never thought capable. He was battling and warring on and was not going to give in to the pugnacious entity.

One of the boys behind Cecilia picked up a rock the size of his hand. In a spontaneous reaction, he threw it toward the Raggedy Ann doll. The boy next to him did the same. He was older, and his rocks were much larger.

A barrage of rocks smashed into the shrub, one after the other, breaking all the branches and smashing the Raggedy Ann doll to pieces. Cecilia slowly regained control of Archie and started to pull him back out of the grips of the evil hands.

Archie's mother was alerted to the attack and scrambled toward them as she dodged playground equipment and uneven turf, nearly losing her footing.

Running behind her was Digger, holding a metal rod, ready to fight off the virulent entity.

The malicious evil realized that it was now under the prowling eyes of too many people and needed to retreat under the cover of darkness. It let go of Archie's ankle while dropping the broken Raggedy Ann doll onto the ground. The devious, evil scoundrel left like a snorting pig, not wanting to be discovered and lose its shroud of anonymity. Witnesses could hear the retreating evil breaking branches and plodding vegetation as it fled the scene.

Cecilia and her mother took Archie into their arms, hugging and kissing him. It had been a close call, and had Cecilia and the boys not reacted quickly enough, Archie would have been lost to the evil crew, perhaps even his sister, too, while trying to save him.

"What happened to you, Archie?" asked the mother, smothering him with hugs while in tears from the ordeal.

He was frightened and unable to speak, stuttering words that did not make sense.

"Something grabbed him in the shrub," said Cecilia, who was sobbing. "His ankles are bleeding, Mum."

Digger had a close look at the injury. "Bloody hell, it's a nasty bite. Some feral animal, I reckon, clawed into him." He had a closer look. "But it doesn't look like the bite of an animal." He picked up the boy and said, "Let's take him to first aid, and if need be, to the hospital in Payneham."

Digger looked back into the shrub as he held Archie. He could see the Raggedy Ann doll in pieces and the broken branches surrounding it.

Was it a wild dog? he thought.

Once he had taken care of Archie and made sure he was in good hands, he was committed to going back the next morning to inspect what was behind the shrub, get some clues, a lead on what attacked the boy. The pioneering village was scheduled to open in a week, and it had to be safe.

Like any small country town, events like these got around quickly in the community. Archie and his family were locals, and they knew people, so gossip would be rife, meaning the pioneering village could be doomed before it officially opened its doors.

The next day, around midday, Digger waited for Clarisse at the front of the motel.

"G'day, luv. Sorry I'm late. Had an issue at the pioneering village, and this one was a bit iffy."

Clarisse jumped into the passenger side and slammed the door. "I heard about the boy—everyone's talking about it."

"Dead set? Geez, word gets around quick." He put on his sunnies. "I know I was supposed to take you yesterday, but I had to assist with the boy. The mother was going bonkers," said Digger. He still appeared rattled after the events of the previous day.

"I don't blame her. It sounds like something weird happened." Clarisse adjusted her seat belt.

"The boy is doing okay; some deep wounds to his ankle area, but he's all bandaged up now."

"Do you know what it was that attacked him?" Clarisse wasted no time getting to the point.

"Maybe a wild dog?" Digger shrugged. "But they are usually shy creatures and don't hang around when there are lots of people about."

Clarisse nodded and did not comment straight away.

He pointed to the only gas station for a hundred miles. "Need to go to the servo—running low on gas." He looked straight at Clarisse and said, "Can you give me the cooler in the back? It's going to be stinking hot again; might get a couple of cold ones. Wanna drink, luv?"

"Sure, thanks. A bottle of cold iced tea."

Besides the motel, the gas station was the only other place with a semblance of activity in Old Tailem Town.

Even though it was a warm day, Digger had not

repaired the air conditioning, preferring to drive with the windows down. It did not bother Clarisse, because she liked to smell the fresh country air, the eucalyptus trees mixed with the smell of the Australian shrubs—bottlebrush and the wattles. It created a unique concoction of fragrance that made you feel calm, at best. It could explain why the locals took everything one step at a time, and Digger was no exception.

"She'll be right, mate. No worries." That was his usual expression.

Clarisse opted to step out the car and wait for Digger while leaning against the driver's side door.

"Here you go, luv. Cold iced tea, as you requested," said Digger when he came out of the gas station.

"Oh, thanks." Clarisse grabbed the icy-cold bottle, juggling it from one side to the other.

Digger smiled as Clarisse finally acclimated to the temperature and took a sip.

"Ready to go see Shamy?" he asked.

"Sure, but I want to ask you something about Payneham and the circus first."

"Sure, luv. What would you like to know?"

"Sometimes, I feel like I'm not getting the whole picture of what happened here in 1935."

Digger was unusually quiet yet nodded several times.

"The locals here are like that … They are bush people, ya know."

"I mean you, Digger."

"Bloody mozzies!" He slapped his face more than once. "This place is full of them." He seemed to be avoiding her question.

"Digger, you haven't told me everything about what happened seventy-five years ago."

"Fair dinkum, luv, I try to stay out of the supernatural stuff. Some things are best left alone."

"But the paranormal tours you run, there is a sense of mystique in those."

"Oh yeah, you have a good point there. But that's business; it's different. I saw an opportunity, and I took it." Digger stepped into the car and waved at Clarisse. "Come on, luv. Shamy's waiting, and we're already late."

Digger turned on the engine and did his usual burst of acceleration, leaving a plume of dust behind. Everyone knew him at the servo, and they looked on and laughed.

Clarisse did not press him any further on the topic, sensing his reluctance. Perhaps her catchup with Shamy would bring an opportunity to dig further into the town's history.

Shamy sat on the porch, waiting for Clarisse to

arrive. Staring into the distance, he gave the impression that he was lost in his own world. Always dressed in black, whether it was trousers and a shirt or a long robe, if you didn't know him, you would think he belonged to a religion. He was trying hard to be non-conformist and regarded himself different from everyone else.

"I'm not sure why he asked to see you again. The man would leap over mountains to stay away from people," said Digger.

He knew Shamy well enough to know it was not a regular afternoon tea visit. He didn't operate that way. There had to be a compelling reason. Shamy never acted spontaneously, and every encounter had a purpose that went beyond an everyday chat. Therefore, Digger wasn't entirely sure what to expect.

"Go with the flow and let Shamy lead the conversation," he advised Clarisse.

She nodded, not saying a word as she prepared to step out of the car.

"Try not to preempt him or predict what he's going to say." Digger was trying hard to make sure her visit would be helpful. "See where the conversation takes you."

Clarisse thought that was good advice. She was not sure how to start the conversation with Shamy, as he was hard to predict. Depending on his mood, she was ready with many questions lingering in her mind about Old Tailem's past. Mysteries about the supernatural elements that were holding the town together from the demonic thuggery of the evil crew.

Shamy leaned forward and gently took hold of Clarisse's hand. The incense filled the air with a mystique that only added to the supernaturalism that clattered the porch—Byzantine crosses and ornaments from a period long gone. Yet, they still had a place in this time, representing Shamy's ritualistic personality.

"Are you ready for another one?" asked Shamy.

Clarisse knew what he meant—back to another time and place, a flashback to the kidnapping of the girl.

"Is there any point going back there again?"

"Remember, I said we missed things the first time? I have gone back several times to find clues, but I have exhausted all my observations." Shamy rubbed her hand with a sacred ointment, pressing on it in a circular motion with his index finger.

"But I am not as strong as you, metaphysically," she said.

"How do you think I learned?" Shamy kept rubbing her hand until Clarisse started to feel calm and slipped into a mild state of meditation. "Fresh eyes, luv. You will see things I haven't noticed. This way, we find its weaknesses."

Clarisse went back to the same place as before, in detail. Although, this time, it was more intense. She could feel the cold air and smell the eucalyptus from the trees. There was also the same rotting smell she had encountered in the church—a potassium and magnesium discharge used by old-fashioned photographers. She shivered and covered her mouth with her right hand, gulping from the evasive stench.

In front of her was the girl, screaming, being ripped away through the flowerbed and into the dense shrub. She kicked viciously while facing upward with her back to the ground, each push of her legs more violent than the last as she tried to fight off the evil.

"Uncle, help me!" she kept repeating, her voice rising to the stars as it filled the empty void. Nothingness lay waiting.

Clarisse tried running toward her, but it made no difference; each attempt resulted in the flashback spinning her around with every step. It would become a blurry image until she stood still.

Lying underneath the shrub was a Raggedy Ann doll with red and blue clothing. At one point, she thought the doll was trying to communicate with the demon, as its mouth moved several times.

Was the Raggedy Ann doll used to lure kids? A ruse that sucked young children into making their way toward the awaiting demon? Smiling and saying a few encouraging words to raise the level of curiosity? How would a child react to a Raggedy Ann speaking to them?

Clarisse heard the thump of a door and turned her focus behind her. It was Digger, bolting out through the back door of a house, running fast, panic-stricken, as he watched his niece being dashed away into the murky darkness. Clarisse put both hands over her eyes, unable to stand it anymore.

It's Digger's niece, she thought. The flashback had hit home. The pain of the past had struck the only person in Old Tailem Town who she had entrusted and come to know as a reliable member of the community.

Digger raced toward his niece, frantic, desperate to save her from the clasps of the demon who was winning over the taking of the child as it started to sap her energy, her fighting spirit deteriorating through sheer exertion. The girl was dragged more deeply into the shrub, her screams of help filling the empty void as they faded into the night and her feet disappeared behind the dense bush.

Digger ran around the shrub frantically, like a mad man, looking for her, but he found nothing but a

Raggedy Ann doll. It was in pieces, as though it had been torn apart by a raging machete of evil.

He continued scouring the shrub for his niece, jumping over logs and scratching himself against underlying branches. He felt no physical pain now. Looking through the smallest of gaps between trees and underneath cavities, it was an intense search, heart thumping and adrenaline rich.

"Where are you? Julie, where are you?" He called her name repeatedly until he had no voice left and collapsed into a bed of leaves, exhausted. He was in tears with his hands over his head, knowing he had lost her to a demonic force.

Oh yes, Digger was aware of the evil that lurked within the town and its preference for children his niece's age. He was a beaten man, but pledged to God that, one day, he would find her, no matter what it took.

Clarisse lost contact with the flashback and returned to the present. Shamy was standing directly in front of her, looking on to make sure she did not lose her balance—a common reaction to the flashback.

"What did you see, luv? Anything of interest?" Shamy was keen to find out if there were any observations, clues, or hidden messages.

Clarisse did not respond right away as she adjusted to

the present and her mind refocused. She had been on an emotional spin. "I saw a Raggedy Ann doll."

"Can you describe it?'

"Well … it was blue and red with a big smile." She paused again to recall the image. "But it was torn in two pieces. That's right; it was laying on the ground and left behind."

Shamy scratched his long beard and looked directly into Clarisse's solid brown eyes. "They forgot to take it?"

"It's a clue, I guess, but I can't make anything of it."

"Yes, luv, I know you're feeling shit-scared about the experience, but I need you to think harder. Focus … What else did you see?"

"Do I need to go through it all over again? Isn't the doll enough?"

"Bloody oath, there's more. There are things I did not see. There are things you did not see the first time. What else? Tell me," Shamy demanded.

"I saw Digger … It was his niece, wasn't it?"

Shamy had not expected Clarisse to see Digger in the flashback, as it would require a lot of explanations.

He stood there, like a figurine, without uttering a word.

"Well, it's Digger or not?" Clarisse insisted.

Shamy turned his back on Clarisse and walked

toward the shed slowly, ignoring her question.

"Crickey!" he exclaimed, wanting to avoid the conversation. "What the demon leaves behind in clues, it carelessly makes up for by throwing in a decoy. Bringing in something else—a controversy that will open old wounds. It was like tit for tat and a warning not to mess around."

The demon had manipulated the flashback to his advantage. He was aware of Shamy's powers—the ability to go back and retrieve information—and there was nothing it could do to stop him.

Clarisse was not going to let Shamy walk away that quickly. She followed him to the shed at a brisk walk, determined to get answers.

"Are you going to respond to my question or not? You asked me to participate in the flashback, and all you can do is walk away?" Clarisse had her hands on her hips, staring directly at him with intent.

Shamy stopped in his tracks and turned around. "For God's sake, you can't say anything to him. He will have another nervous breakdown." Shamy waved Clarisse toward the entrance of his shed. "One word about his niece and the memory will knock him about. He lost his family over it—his wife, home, job, everything dear to him."

Clarisse kept walking toward Shamy, feeling tense.

He kneeled next to the altar, and Clarisse joined him, having taken a couple of deep breaths and calmed down by now. There was positive energy, although subtle and not as vibrant as before, with different undertones.

"You have been to the church again?" asked Shamy.

"Yes, and—"

"You don't have to explain yourself. I know you touched the sacred stone, the *carbonados*."

His intuition caught her by surprise. *How could he know I entered the crypt? Nobody was there at the time*, she thought.

"How do you know?" asked Clarisse.

"We are connected, like an alarm system. I know when the evil crew is running about the church, trying to take over, trying to defeat the power of the stone." Shamy looked at Clarisse with his penetrating, dark-brown eyes, cryptic and almost magical. "I know they confronted you and failed."

"They couldn't get near the stone, that beautiful black gem with all that energy. I have never experienced that feeling." Clarisse turned to Shamy.

"So, what's this sacred power you have?"

"Next time, luv. You've had a big day." He waved goodbye to her and smiled without uttering a word. He was not going to tell her everything at once. It would have to wait for their next encounter, if there was one. It was about building enough trust with Shamy. There was no shortcut; it would take as long as needed. Would he ask her to come back and perform another flashback? Look for more chinks in the evil crew's armor?

Clarisse was well in tune with demonic behavior and understood every dark spirit had weak spots, vulnerabilities that could be exposed and taken advantage of. Shamy's strategy was to leverage off any weaknesses he could find and exploit it. Clarisse had learned from her previous encounters with dark spirits that, to beat them, you needed to understand their history, motivations, and who was controlling their actions—their purpose and goals in the transient world. It was like a business plan for demons.

She accepted demons operated in niches with a team-based approach, although a contradiction. Presumably, they had to trust each other to survive. Perhaps the teams were created by opportunity—being at the right place at the right time—or simple ambition and entrepreneurialism. They needed to satisfy their master to get ahead in the hierarchy and to stay relevant. That meant coming up with plans of evil manifestations that entertained the underworld and their protégés. Demons had to make a name for themselves to get ahead like in any organized structure.

The drive back to the motel lacked the usual banter between Digger and Clarisse. Neither was in the mood for talking. It felt as though Digger had sensed something had taken place close to his heart. He behaved differently and was not himself, focused only on driving back to Old Tailem Town. A part of her wanted to tell him everything—throw it into the open and come clean. Another part stuck to her promise not to mention the flashback, heeding Shamy's request to stay clear of it.

Getting snippets of information from the locals and being drip-fed was frustrating. They wanted her to dig up information but not all of it, preferring to keep a lid on it when it became too much. Clarisse had more questions than answers.

Frustrating as it was, however, it was not the first time she had encountered such behavior amongst tightknit communities. She was an outsider with no connection or ties to the local community, so why should they trust and grant her the privilege of knowing in thirty minutes what they had learned over a hundred years?

Her best option was to return to Giselle at the circus camp. They were not locals connected to the hereditary evil of Old Tailem Town. And maybe they would speak up without Digger present. It was worth a try. She would ask Harry to take her there the next morning.

A storm had settled overhead, and the cracking sound of thunder created an unusual Outback display. It was much louder here than in the city; a rawness and sense of wilderness unmatched by the more urban, populated areas. Clarisse could feel the intensity as the lightning flashed through the windows of the motel with a brilliant light show that caused the electricity to flicker momentarily. The motel lights purred with each lightning strike with a hissing sound.

The preparations for opening day were well underway, and many people involved in setting up the town's infrastructure were in attendance—electricians, concreters, systems and communications experts, and the marketing team with their fancy photographic equipment. Some photographers had heard about the paranormal tours and had brought their infrared devices and specialized sound equipment for a bit of fun. Who knew? They might pick up the sounds of a ghost wailing in the background or the image of an energy source traversing the room like a lost soul. Whatever the case, these guys wanted to catch a real-life ghost and make it the main attraction for the pioneering village—a great marketing scheme.

The marketing group scribbled a motto on their whiteboard as they fiercely debated the best promotional angle. Circled in large, bold lettering, a catchy phrase caught Clarisse's attention.

Running from evil is not a bad idea … until you realize you can't hide.

Dinner was the same as usual—the same bad food and poor service, to boot. If the level of service was ignored, her and Harry could become accustomed to accepting the inferior business standards as a regular practice. A business like this would go broke in a big city, as the city folk were more demanding on their expectations of service. But Old Tailem was a monopoly, since there was nothing else for a hundred miles. The next motel was in Payneham, and they had heard the establishment there was not much better.

Harry placed a printout of a report that he had obtained in front of Clarisse, impromptu and enthusiastically.

Clarisse jolted from the unexpected thump of paper ricocheting off the timber table. "What's this?"

"Well, look what I have found—a medical report connected to the children who went missing from the circus in 1935. It's archival stuff, and I had to pull a few tricks to get it." Harry smiled, standing there like a boy waiting for a pat on the back or a big hug, proud of his investigation and wanting to impress Clarisse. "You were right about one thing," he said.

"And what's that? I'm confused."

"They don't tell you everything around here. I got this report from the Payneham archive office, the same lady who gave us the manifest," said Harry.

"She conveniently forgot about it?"

"Hmm, more than likely, until I pressed her on it and she gave in."

He flicked through the pages until he arrived at the summary report. "Look at this. The children belonged to a religious sect that practiced mind-distorting behaviors. It was the government of South Australia that took custody of these orphans and sent them to the supervised care of the circus."

Clarisse cringed, and her forehead creased as she perused the document. "It says they suffered psychiatric trauma and conditioning."

"Yep. And how coincidental that they all disappeared at the same time?" Harry flicked over to the last page. "See this?" He pointed to a paragraph on the page. "The article mentions Giselle."

"Oh, it can't be." In the article, Giselle was already an adult. "That would make her over one hundred years old. Maybe it's a different Giselle?"

"Well, here is her photo from 1935. A remarkable resemblance, if that is the case," said Harry.

Clarisse picked up the photo to get a closer look, peering over the image to make sure. "It does look like her … I mean, it's almost identical."

Harry sighed and nodded. "I told you. Anyway, we are making an impromptu visit tomorrow morning." He took hold of Clarisse's hand. "Let's see what the old spiritual healer has to say this time."

They both looked at each other, astonished by their find. The children had been troubled souls before they had joined the sanctuary of the circus. The demon had handpicked them, and it had made for easy pickings. Perfect for a new gang.

The drive to the circus next to the Billabong took about fifteen minutes. They were in no hurry to break any speed records as Harry reclined in his seat while resting one arm on the driver's side window. He was cruising, enjoying the country sun and the smell of the native bush.

Although he was a city boy who had grown up in the

hustle and bustle of Sydney, he enjoyed every moment of his time in the Australian bush. It had the distinctive sounds of local birds perched high in the eucalyptus trees. Occasionally, he would stop at the sighting of a koala hugging a branch and eating leaves. These marsupials did not move much, and one had to be careful not to mistake their calmness with their reaction to strangers. They were known to lash out with their sharp claws at people who tried to pat them.

As they made the last turn toward the Billabong, they could see the caravans in the distance. There was some commotion. It appeared they were packing up and getting ready to move on.

"Looks like we got here in time," said Clarisse.

Waiting in front of the main caravan was the mysterious lady dressed in gypsy attire with a tied headscarf—Giselle.

"She must have known we were coming," said Harry.

"Oh yeah. This woman has a sixth sense about her."

Harry parked the vehicle on the gravel area next to where Giselle was standing as he waved to her impulsively. She did not wave back, just stood there, staring at them both with a thoughtful expression. She already knew why they had come to see her. It was more than a gut feel.

Clarisse stepped out of the car first and walked over to Giselle at a steady pace with the documents in hand—the Payneham archives.

"Looks like you're getting ready to leave soon," said Clarisse.

"Oh yes, my dear. We are leaving first thing tomorrow morning." Giselle folded her arms across her chest and tilted her head slightly. She had a curious look, her nose screwed up like a squirrel. It was not the sort of welcome they were expecting. "I know why you're here."

"You know?" responded Clarisse.

"Let me put it this way: I had a strong feeling to expect you today."

"Can we talk about something we found? You may be able to provide some clarity."

Giselle did not answer right away. She waited for Harry to step out of the car, and then she pointed to the alfresco table next to her caravan. "We can take a seat over there and talk."

Once seated, they all took turns staring at each other, waiting for someone to start the conversation. Clarisse grew impatient and started first. It would allow her to control the discussion.

"We found this photo at Payneham cemetery … in the archive office. It's a missing piece of the puzzle."

Clarisse laid the photo in front of Giselle. "It looks a lot like you … almost identical, if you ask me."

"When was this taken?"

"Payneham … 1935. And I guess that would make you well over one hundred years old."

"One hundred and ten, to be exact," confirmed Giselle with a smile, proud of her milestone.

Startled by her admission, Clarisse shifted in her chair to release the tension. "One hundred and ten years old! You're probably the oldest person in this country."

"Not probably, my dear; I *am* the oldest by a long shot. I think the next person in line has turned a hundred years old, but I heard she is not well."

"How do you—"

"How do I keep myself alive and healthy?" interrupted Giselle. "Well, that's a secret I can't share with you. It's deeply spiritual and personal."

Annoyed by her attitude, Clarisse decided to cut to the chase. "We found in the archives that the missing children came from a religious sect. They had problems … demons of their own to deal with."

"So, you know about that, too?"

"It's not easy trying to get information from people around here; we had to go looking," said Clarisse.

"Well, they came into our care because it was my job

to remove the demonic curse from the children. That was the unofficial version. The official version was that we became their foster parents."

"And …?"

"I guess you're asking if I was successful?"

There was a deep silence as they all pretended to ignore each other. The conversation was becoming uncomfortable.

"Maybe we should leave?" interrupted Harry.

"No, I will tell you." Giselle put her hand on the photo and closed her eyes.

"The demon was strong, and I could not defeat it. I knew I was going to lose the children." A teardrop rolled down from Giselle's left eye at the emotional impact of recalling the events. "I did all I could and tried everything. Every day was like going to war—a battleground. I was young and not experienced enough."

"Thank you, Giselle." Clarisse understood the impact the memories was having on Giselle and decided to stop the conversation. "And sorry to trouble you with old memories. I know it's not easy recollecting something so devastating after such a long time."

"I think we should leave, Clarisse," said Harry once more.

As they were heading back to the car, Giselle called

out and said, "It's the same demon, you know—the one you confronted in the church. And it knows you." Giselle held on to her cross with both hands. "Be careful, my dear. It's more powerful than you think, and sinister!"

Clarisse turned around and nodded in acknowledgement, waving goodbye with a slight twist of her hand. She then stepped into the car and asked Harry to drive her back to the motel at Old Tailem Bend.

She glanced in the rearview mirror to find Giselle arguing with Christoff. Something was amiss. Her visit must have upset him.

Clarisse blinked a few times as she tried to focus on them. Then they disappeared out of sight within an instant. It was at least twenty yards to the next caravan— they couldn't have walked that quickly. Too bizarre; she continued to look on, thinking her eyes had played tricks on her. But no, they were gone, like phantoms, just like that.

There were consequences with poking into the history that surrounded Old Tailem Town. The more they dug, the more they found. She had ingrained herself so much in the town's paranormal phenomena that she could not walk away. Clarisse was a spirit hunter and felt the propensity to unlock the evil murkiness that lay beneath. She had announced her intentions to the demon, and now they saw her as a threat. She knew enough that the second wave of evil was underway, the first having ended in 1935.

Opening day was only five days away, where a battle royale between good and evil would play itself out. Clarisse was on the frontline now, and a lot depended on her. But how was she going to muster the town's forces to fight off the devil and his crew? She was in a quandary, but not without hope.

7 DEMON'S LAIR

Clarisse felt a presence behind her. There was a clatter and nervous finger tapping, fingernails in sequence on a wooden surface. She was praying at the church, and it had disrupted her, perhaps deliberately.

The evil crew did not welcome prayers, a homage to a God who only ruffled their determination, as they belonged to the demon of the underworld—their master. She knew it was not Little Charlie; his footsteps were ingrained in her mind like a calling card. Something else was toying with her.

Clarisse heard the tapping again, louder now and with scraping fingernails against polished floorboards, a distinctive sound. A horrible screech sounded then, and she shook her shoulders, a nervous reaction, uncontrollable with a twitching motion. She turned around to inspect the sound, and there it was.

Sitting two rows directly behind her and looking

mocking, confident, and cheeky, portraying a fake, forced, crooked grin, the boy with the angular face looked more terrible closer than in the darkness—a distorted face, gruesome, half-boy and half-demon, animalistic in parts.

Clarisse tried not to overreact or show fear, pretending not to notice his shattered, crumbled appearance.

"So, you are here again, miss. Can't stay away from this house of worship, hey?" said the demon.

"This is not your house, demon, and I can come here whenever I please." Clarisse was defiant.

"Yeah, good point, miss. But it will be mine one day. It's only a matter of time, ya know. A game of patience, and I have been at it for one hundred years ... Now is my time."

Behind the demon stood his crew. They appeared one by one, from out of nowhere. First, it was Little Charlie, holding his rope like a lasso. He was sitting on the altar, cross-legged with baggy, knee-length shorts and messed-up socks. Then appeared a young girl in a crimson dress, caressing a Raggedy Ann doll. It was the same girl who she had encountered in the graveyard, jumping over unmarked headstones. Finally, another girl, not stretching or performing her trapeze act this time, sitting stationary and cross-legged with her index finger pointing below her chin. She had a determined stare with made-up innocence; so fake it was ineffective, as Clarisse could see right through the immaturity. The last of the crew was a young boy on his unicycle, balancing while remaining stationary. It was quite a feat.

"You may want to say hello to my family," said the demon.

"Oh, I have seen them before, especially Little Charlie. He's not from here, you know. You followed me here, didn't you, Charlie?" asked Clarisse.

Little Charlie whisked around his lasso and smiled.

"Yeah, Little Charlie, he's a ripper. Fits in very well since he joined us. Great team member. Might give him an award for his work." The demon smiled cynically.

"You won't win me over with your sarcasm, demon. But tell me one thing; why do you call your crew your family? Aren't you the destroyer of families? A contradiction?"

"I saved them from a life of eternal damnation. I look after them and, in return, they keep me company. They are my friends. Can't live alone, ya know. It can be lonely being a demon, in the same place for over a hundred years with nothing much to do."

"So, you want me to feel sorry for you? You are a

kidnapper—stealing children during the night from their parents so that you can have company. That's how your underworld operates." Clarisse paused before she unleashed on him again. "Your master requires it, doesn't he? It's your pact. You steal the children on his command, and he gets a kick out of it. In return, he allows you to control your patch with your crew, and you get to keep Old Tailem Town."

"Ha, ha … not so fast, miss." The demon could not help laughing as his evil crew joined in the banter. "I guess you're smarter than I thought." He pointed directly toward her and cringed, his bloodshot eyes penetrating beneath his extended forehead. "Yeah, but my master did warn me about you. Said you're rather good at this. Built a bit of a reputation for yourself, hey?"

"I don't think you are here to have a chat. I have been around long enough to know you want something. So, what is it? Cut to the chase."

The demon unleashed a crooked smile and placed his hands on his legs, leaning forward. "I have a proposition for you, miss. You are the first mortal to get into that crypt. No one has ever been able to open it, so that makes you special. Most people would've run out of town by now, yet you're still here."

"What is it, demon?" Clarisse did not want to

become a conversationalist, and she knew the demon's spin.

He paused and looked around the room. "You show me how to get into that crypt and destroy that stone, and I will grant you riches you have never imagined." He lifted his arms in the air. "Maybe you can have your own patch. I hear Payneham is up for grabs. That would make us neighbors."

"You take me for a fool, demon. You think you are the first to play that game with me? Ha." She took a deep breath and looked on.

"You don't need to protect Shamy. He's nothing to you. That fool is stuck in his time warp, but if you can befriend him …?"

"What? Unlock the secret of the *carbonado*s and hand it to you on a platter for a piece of the patch? Power? You offering me Payneham Town?"

"I can give you more. The power of a thousand dreams and anything you want with no master hovering over you. Unlike me, you can operate as a standalone."

Clarisse knew that sometimes it was best to say nothing, to avoid the conversation altogether.

"As I said, miss, think about it carefully. My master might decide to call off my wolves on opening day. Lots of kids are going to be in town. Ha, ha. I won't know where to start. It will be a free-for-all."

Within the space of ten seconds, the evil crew was all gone as quickly as they had appeared.

It was not the first time a demon had tried to make a deal with her. It had happened in Hartley with the phantom in the cellar. She had learned they all were liars—untrustworthy, misleading con artists who never held their word. Because the underworld did not value contracts. Deals were made to be broken. Clarisse had learned a deal could look remarkably attractive by providing a preview to whet your appetite, to lock you in until there was no way out. That was their ploy.

Giselle had warned about the demon and its tricks. She had also mentioned it was more potent than one hundred years ago, and it had learned to fly under the radar, popping up during crucial moments to make a point, frighten you away, or con you into a deal. This demon had learned from its master to be a strategist and to only strike when the iron was hot. There was a place and a time for battles, and this demon played its card close to its chest.

Clarisse could not help feeling that a battle for supremacy was coming. Everything was stacked up nicely for a push by the demon to start their reign of terror. The most significant event in the town's history was happening next week, and families and children would be soaking up the new attractions. Everyone was waiting for it, and the crescendo of evil was patiently sitting on the sidelines, ready to strike.

Shamy had not been willing to tell her everything, tight-lipped about the past and present evil. Why were they keeping the town's evil footprint tucked away? She had so many questions flashing across her mind that it made her feel disadvantaged. She was dealing with a demonic presence with one hand tied behind her back. It was not a good position to be in when a demon had the upper hand.

The devil operated as an evil crew—teamwork and coordination. Old Tailem was fragmented, confused, and disorganized. Digger, Shamy, and even Giselle did not behave as a united front. And, of course, the demon was aware that fragmentation gave it an edge.

It left Shamy as the only weapon against the evil crew. A task too large for one man? Shamy also held on to his family's secrets, unwilling to share it with Clarisse—a magical black stone, a *carbonados*, in a crypt underneath the church, so powerful that the demon and his crew could not withstand it. The demon saw it as a barrier and would do anything to destroy it, even negotiate a deal … a deal with the devil.

Clarisse needed more information on the sacred stone—its origins and how it ended in a bush town in the middle of nowhere. Did she go back to Shamy and put these difficult questions defiantly in front of him and force his hand? Did she need to revisit the crypt and look for other clues? Would Digger have some knowledge and provide her with a lead? It was like a secret society, a holy order that went back centuries, that only a chosen few had the privilege of knowing.

Clarisse had a lot of thinking to do and not much time before opening day.

Digger was waiting outside the church, ready to drive Clarisse back to the motel.

"G'day, luv. It's been a ripper of a day."

Clarisse stepped into the front passenger side and smiled. "Thanks for giving me a ride, as always."

"Yeah, with all the people in town at the moment, I feel like a shuttle bus!" Digger laughed while waving his hand to scare the flies away. It was your typical Aussie salute.

Clarisse wound down her window to breathe in the scent of the bush. "How is that boy doing? Is he okay now?"

"Oh yes, he's all bandaged up and doing fine …

except his mother, who is still a wreck." He looked toward Clarisse with a poignant look. "They reckon it was dingoes. But between you and me, it's all bullshit."

Clarisse could see he was in the mood for letting on to something.

"Ya see, those bloody dogs couldn't have pierced him on both ankles like that." Digger pulled out a cigarette while he held on to the steering wheel with the other hand. "They looked like the marks of two hands—long nails cutting into the skin—not a dog, for God's sake!"

"Yes, but who would attempt to kidnap a boy with so many people around?" She folded her arms and looked straight ahead, impervious to any rationale.

"That's a ripper of a question: the million-dollar one. But I'm going to have to pass because I don't know." He took a puff of his cigarette with an unusually deep inhale, as though he needed it. Clarisse could see Digger was on edge.

"You don't have to answer; I'm thinking out loud." Clarisse paused for a moment as a family of kangaroos jumped around in the open field as they drove past the animal sanctuary.

"Gotta be careful with these roos. They jump in front of you at night, blinded by the car lights, silly animals." He slowed down the car so Clarisse could get a better look. "Oh crikey, I nearly forgot. Shamy asked if you could pass by tomorrow."

"I thought he was upset with me?"

"Oh, he is a silly bugger sometimes. Cannot handle people and their questions. He told me to say he was sorry for his behavior the other day."

"Should be fine, Digger. I will check with Harry tonight."

"He was speaking gobbledygook yesterday, and he was in one of those moods again. Always cracking the shits." He looked directly at Clarisse, eagle-eyed. "He said something about a boy called Little Charlie. Do ya know him?"

Clarisse gulped then spat her water out the window, surprised Digger had learned about Little Charlie.

"Are ya all right, luv?" asked Digger

"Yeah, a fly went into my mouth."

"Bloody insects are everywhere this time of year. Found one in my tucker yesterday!"

"Yes, I know Little Charlie, but not in the way that you think. It's more spiritual."

"No drama, luv. Ya don't need to explain it to me if it's personal. Thought I'd let ya know he mentioned it."

Clarisse tried to change the topic. "I'll send you a message once I have spoken to Harry. Can you suggest a time for tomorrow?"

"Shamy's useless in the morning. Sleeps in because he's always up late. Heaven knows what he does all night."

Digger dropped Clarisse off at the front of the motel with a sudden halt as the car spun forty-five degrees. "How about two p.m. tomorrow then?"

She closed the car door, noticing a Raggedy Ann doll in the back seat. She wanted to say something, but he was in a rush, off to another paranormal tour in Old Tailem, his second for the night. However, the Raggedy Ann doll had become synonymous with evil, a tool used by the demon to lure children to a life of spiritual nothingness. It perplexed her.

What was Digger doing with a Raggedy Ann doll? The incident with the boy a couple of days ago involved the same doll and similar tactics—using it as a demon magnet.

She bid Digger goodbye and thanked him once more for the ride. "See you tomorrow at two p.m.," she confirmed.

Digger winked and smiled as he waved goodbye. Then he burst off with a sudden jolt as the car skidded onto the main street, accelerating like a hot rod. She could hear the roar of his modified engine as onlookers watched on.

The evening passed quietly with the usual dinner in the motel restaurant. They had become conditioned and resigned to the lousy menu. It was either the steak, chips, and eggs, or go hungry.

"How's the project going, Harry?" Clarisse asked as she settled back in her chair.

"We are nearly done. Hooked up the internet today." He poured a glass a beer into his chilled glass then gulped a quarter of it.

"Thirsty?"

"Is it always warm in Old Tailem Town, or maybe it's that time of year?"

Clarisse smiled. "You know, Harry, I just realized I have been tagging along with you for the last year with your work."

"You don't like it?" Harry queried.

"Sometimes I think I'm a burden because I don't work or do anything—I'm not being productive."

Harry paused. "Think of it as a tour of rural Australia. You get to see the real Australian Outback." He took another sip of his beer. "Better than any bus tour, don't you think?."

Clarisse smiled. "That part of it I really like."

"Look, you're not a burden on me. I love the company, and it can get lonely in these places."

She nodded. "I hope you don't mind me researching the towns."

"Oh, you do more than that. You get right into it … with the paranormal side, I mean." Harry crossed his arms and looked directly at Clarisse. "I hope you're taking notes. I'm thinking you could write a blog and have it published in the Philippines."

"That's a thought. Maybe I will start my paranormal blog about Australian ghost towns. I bet my friends and family would like reading about it."

They both nodded and agreed. Harry thought it was a great idea and continued their conversation about the blog until they were the last people out of the restaurant.

"G'day, luv. Ready for another visit to the great master?" Digger asked the next morning. He was on time and prepared for the drive to Shamy's home.

"How was your paranormal show last night?" asked Clarisse, stepping into the front passenger side and winding down the window. "Looks like another warm day ahead."

"The show went great. Record turnout. Might have to find an extra hand if the numbers keep growing like this!" He gave her a telling look.

Clarisse laughed. "No, I'm not looking for a job. Forget it!"

"Ha, ha. Ya know it would be perfect for ya. Can't think of anyone who knows their spirituality like you. And you present well. The blokes will like ya!" Digger smiled while nodding, trying to coax her. "Go on, luv; might be a good way to spend the summer and make some good money."

"I will think about it, but don't hold your breath."

Digger leaned over toward the glove box. "Better put on my sunnies. The sun's glare is pretty strong this time of day."

"Do you know anyone who has lost a child in Old Tailem in the last fifteen years? Like what almost happened to the boy a few days ago?" It was the question that had been burning inside her since the day they had tried to snatch Archie.

Digger turned his head and looked straight toward the road, focused on his cigarette in one hand while controlling the steering wheel in the other. She had hit a raw nerve.

"Well, Digger? Are you going to ignore my question?"

"Fair dinkum, luv, of course I do. I have been in this

town all my life, seen a lot of things." He took a deep puff of his cigarette then exhaled out the window. "Bringing it up isn't going to help. We forgot about it. It took me years to get over it. Some people around here still haven't and cling on to the memory."

Clarisse had known the question would be greeted with a level of remorse but also avoidance.

"What about you? Did you lose someone close to you?"

"Ya know something, luv, don't ya? I could see it in yer eyes after yer last meeting with Shamy."

"Yes, I saw something …"

"During yer meditation, or flashbacks, as he calls them?"

"Yes …"

"Then you already know. She was my niece. I never found her. A search party, police investigations—we threw everything at it … but nothing."

"And the Raggedy Ann doll?"

"It belonged to her. And to be honest, luv, I don't know where she got it, but I think Shamy wants to find out, thanks to you."

Clarisse remained tight-lipped, hoping it would encourage Digger to elaborate further.

"That bloody mongrel that took her … if I ever find

who did it, I will tear him to shreds." Digger was an Outback man and as tough as they came, but the thought of his niece was enough to bring watery eyes.

"It's okay, Digger. I can feel the pain, too. We don't need to go into this any further."

They arrived at Shamy's residence on time. Digger knew he was a stickler for time, which made no sense. Everything was slower in the bush, and the townsfolk played out their day in their own time. It was one of Shamy's pet hates, although they were at a loss as to what kept him busy all day.

Shamy greeted them from the front porch, sipping on a cup of tea, with a thick book in his hand. It looked ancient, like a collector's item, with a black leather cover and the sign of a Byzantine cross embossed in red. The back of the book contained another embossed image—a *carbonado* in the form of a flower and the outer-lying sepals.

"Here you are, mate. The Raggedy Ann," said Digger, handing it to him.

Shamy acknowledged it with a smile. "This is going to help."

"What ya going to do with a doll?" Digger was mystified.

Shamy set it down on a chair. "Clarisse and I are

going to tap into its energy with a flashback."

"You mean, *another* one of those flashbacks?" asked Clarisse.

"Well, this time we will join forces, go there together." Shamy was in the mood for a spiritual face-off.

"Can you do that?"

Shamy brushed his long, curly hair away from his face then caressed his beard. "With you, I can. You're strong enough."

"I will go and feed the champion in the barn," said Digger. He had a prized Angus bull for breeding, a local blue-ribbon champion two years in a row at the agricultural show.

"Clarisse, I need some information before we go into the flashback. It's for our safety." Shamy opened his notebook, where he usually scribbled observations and thoughts during his prayer time. "Little Charlie, you brought him here. Or, let me rephrase that—he followed you from Hartley."

"Well, I didn't know …"

Shamy took another sip of his tea. "Oh, sorry for being so rude. Would you like some herbal tea? Grown in the local area, ya know."

She acknowledged Shamy's offer and poured herself a cup. "Smells delightful. It has a unique fragrance."

Shamy smiled. "I thought you would like it."

He waited for Clarisse to take a sip then continued. "You can run, but you can't hide."

"What do you mean?"

"You defeated Little Charlie's master, but he followed you. You can't run from evil once it latches on to you."

She took another sip of tea then sat back in the chair with her legs crossed. "How do you know all this?"

"I am a shaman; the power is handed down for generations. I can see evil coming, and evil can see me. A gift from God, but sometimes I wish I never had this burden. It does wear ya down, luv."

"Has it affected the town? Little Charlie's presence, I mean?"

"Yes, luv. He brought his know-how—his bag of tricks from the other phantom—and teamed up with the evil crew. It made them stronger. Plus, he knows a lot about you."

"I think I'm beginning to understand. But he's a kid."

"Kids mature very quickly in the world of demons. He might be young, innocent, and you may feel sorry for him, but he does not feel sorry for you." Shamy took another sip of tea then placed his book on the table in front of him. "Little Charlie has joined a team of evil, with the opportunity to start running amok again—a reinvigorated evil crew."

"And what about this Raggedy Ann doll? What's that all about?"

"My belief is something evil brought it here a long time ago. It got passed down a few times, became a tool of the demon in Old Tailem. And what a perfect way to draw an unsuspecting child into your trap."

"What do you plan to do with this doll?" The Raggedy Ann was on the chair next to her. She did not want to touch it, aware of its opposing energy.

Shamy smiled. "The doll will take us to its place of origin; show us where it came from—its original master. Are you ready?"

"What? Right here, on the porch?"

"There are no rules with flashbacks, luv, as long as you're not in the middle of a crowded street or restaurant, if you know what I mean."

"Okay, Shamy, let's find out about this evil Raggedy Ann. I'm curious."

Her confidence inspired Shamy to join her in the flashbacks. He needed someone strong and decisive, able to confront darkness without falling into a heap, determined and headstrong.

Shamy took hold of Clarisse's hand and diverted all his energy to her palms. "Are you ready?" he asked again.

"Yes, I'm ready." Clarisse nodded and looked down at her palms.

Shamy went into prayer with an orthodox chant.

"O Lord Jesus Christ, our God, the true and living way, be thou, O Master, my companion, guide, and guardian during my journey; deliver and protect me from all danger, misfortune, and temptation, that being so defended by Thy divine power, that I may have a peaceful and prosperous journey and arrive safely at my destination. For in thee, I put my trust and hope, and to thee, together with thy Eternal Father, and the All Holy Spirit, I ascribe all praise, honor, and glory, now and ever, and unto ages of ages. Amen."

Clarisse fell into a meditated state as she had done before. Her mind wandered before landing on the same porch in front of Shamy's house forty years in the past. She looked ahead toward the gravel driveway as an old, red pickup rattled into the front entrance, puffing black smoke and bouncing. The pickup had seen better days and struggled to make the most basic of maneuvers.

A man in his thirties stepped out of the truck with a limp. He was wearing a checkered shirt, dusty, straight-leg country jeans with a rip down the side, and work boots with worn outsoles. He had a floral red gypsy headband tied around his forehead and studded gold earrings.

She looked closely to capture a clear image of his face—a pointed nose and angular face that protruded from his flattened forehead. She had seen this face before, but in a different time.

Yes, it's him. The demon, she thought.

She looked straight into its eyes—bloodshot, unnatural, and penetrating, which only reinforced her opinion. It was the same demon that was running mad in modern-day Old Tailem Town.

The man walked to the front door in an agitated state, each step a strain on his ugly face. Something was bothering him.

He knocked on the door several times with his cane until Shamy, a ten-year-old boy, answered the door next to his father. The door wide open, his father held on to Shamy as he greeted the man.

"G'day, mate. Sorry to bother you this time of day, but I'm passing through town and thought you might need a ranch hand for a couple of days." The man removed his Jacaru hat and nodded. "I'm at your service, mate, and can do anything on a farm. I'm an experienced hand."

Shamy's dad looked on silently, sensing something

odd about the man. "What happened to your eyes? They are red, bloodshot. You're not on the grog?"

"Nah, mate. Dust in my eyes, and they flare up sometimes, ya know?" He paused and looked at Shamy with an unnatural grin.

"I don't have any work for ya here, but old man Cleg down the road is looking for someone. Two miles that way."

"Oh, mate, thanks for your recommendation. I would like to give your boy something. I got it at the local fair in Payneham while doing some work there. I don't have any need for it. I don't have a missus or kids." He took out a Raggedy Ann doll from his bag and held it in front of Shamy. It was different from the red and blue colors of the other dolls in Old Tailem Town. This one was dressed in green and white stripes.

Shamy was about to take it from the man when his father put his hand out to stop him. Then Shamy put his head down and said, "Sorry, I don't take gifts from strangers."

Shamy's father looked into the man's bloodshot eyes with a sharp focus, eagle-eyed and unrelenting, now definitely sensing something was not right. This man was not who he claimed to be.

The man nodded then said goodbye before he made

his way to the pickup, holding his Raggedy Ann doll in one hand and maintaining his balance with a walking stick in the other. Then he stopped suddenly at the gate and turned around. "I don't need this doll anymore, mate. Maybe give it to someone else? I'm sure there are lots of kids in town who would like it." He put the Raggedy Ann on the fence post, adjusted it, and then walked to the pickup.

Clarisse looked closely at the green and white Raggedy Ann from her meditated state. To her surprise, its face turned toward the man, grinned, and winked. It was possessed, a conduit of evil.

The doll was left behind to play its master's part in spreading its evil like a Trojan horse. They had found the pipe of sin that was ripping through modern-day Old Tailem Town.

The flashback ended, and Clarisse returned from her meditated state, as did Shamy.

"I remember that doll …" he said. "It meant nothing at the time. I was a boy."

Clarisse shook her head, dizzy, as was usually the case after a deep meditation. "Do you remember where the doll ended up?"

"My dad didn't want me to have it. He said it was cursed, and the man was a demon." Shamy sat back in his chair and stared into the distance. The memory of his father, who he had loved and admired so much, brought a tear to his eyes. "I remember my dad telling me a story that demons come in all sizes and packages, and that I had to be on my guard, learn to spot them. Sometimes they pose as innocent people with gifts when, unbeknownst, they are trying to destroy everything dear to you. A broken marriage, sick child, financial ruin—suddenly things go bad, and you don't know the source of your bad luck."

"Your father was a very spiritual man. I could feel his connection with God very strongly," said Clarisse.

Shamy sat quietly for a moment, his hand poised over his forehead. He appeared to be thinking of something important.

"What is it, Shamy?" asked Clarisse.

"That doll ... We need to find it. It's still in the town. I remember taking it to our local priest at the time. He had a storage room at the back of the church with all the unwanted stuff—bits and pieces that nobody wanted, mainly discarded old toys."

"Is it still there?"

"Nobody has touched that storage room in decades. I'm the only one who has the keys to the place." Shamy stood up, feeling reinvigorated. "When the last priest left town and the church stood abandoned, they gave the keys to my father. He became the keeper. No one wanted to look after it. It was finally passed down to me after he died." Shamy looked at Clarisse and took hold of her hand. "We need to find that doll, luv. I reckon it's still there … in that storage room."

Clarisse nodded, agreeing.

The Raggedy Ann doll was an evil conduit, and by finding and destroying it before opening day meant the demon had one less significant weapon in its arsenal.

Contrary to old wives' tales, it was not uncommon for demons to possess physical objects, like chairs, mirrors, and dolls, to name a few. These objects typically played a part in attracting unsuspecting individuals to their fate.

8 TOWN HALL MEETING

The church at Old Tailem was full, so only standing room remained for those arriving late. It was the only place big enough to hold around fifty people in one location. Investors, businessowners, mums and dads that had invested in the opening of the pioneering village had come to hear Digger speak about canceling opening day.

As much as he had resisted the temptation to call a meeting, because he felt others would mock him, thanks to Clarisse, he had found the courage to confront them. He was the chairperson of the Old Tailem Town Committee and the leading entrepreneur. His paranormal tours were the main attraction bringing tourists into town from off the beaten track. They relied on him for their business survival and had no choice but to hear his point of view.

Clarisse decided to sit in the last aisle, next to the trapdoor that led to the crypt. She was amazed at how people walked over it without noticing, unbeknownst that underneath contained one of the most sacred stones on Earth.

Across the aisle was Kezza, the motel owner. She couldn't help staring at Clarisse with an intense look, obviously annoyed that she had influenced Digger to call this meeting. Shamy was seated in the aisle behind her, left by himself like a misfit. Harry latched on to that quickly and introduced himself to Shamy, taking the seat next to him.

Everyone liked talking to Harry, and Shamy was no exception. He even managed to pull a smile from him a couple of times, something Clarisse had never managed.

"Can I call everyone to order?" shouted Digger as he stood at the altar, tall and dignified. There was another side to Digger, and that was his serious side, the entrepreneurial businessman, not the larrikin who Clarisse often encountered on her drives out of town in his car.

The room became silent, and rumblings thinned out as they prepared for Digger to open the discussion.

"Thank you all for being here. And I reckon this is a great turnout for the town. I see people here that I haven't seen for yonks—years—and some old folk who have been here for generations."

He had the Raggedy Ann doll next to him on a table.

People peered at it, unsure of its purpose.

"I have called you here as interested parties, businessowners, and financiers for the pioneering village and its opening next week. I am going to discuss with you my reasons for recommending its delay."

There was hissing throughout the room as the townsfolk whispered to each other and pointed at the doll.

"Yeah, yeah, I know you have all spent a lot of your own money on this project, and I understand more than anyone in this room how important it is we start making a profit. I get it. But five days ago, a local boy was attacked outside this church near the graveyard. The investigation remains inconclusive, but it was not a rogue dingo that comes out at night. Someone tried to steal a child from their family, and we have been concerned ever since."

Everyone in the room nodded. They all knew about what had happened to the local boy.

"The only thing I found was a Raggedy Ann doll, like this one. And for those of you who did not grow up or have parents who came from the area, this doll is a clue … It has been with us before." Digger paused and took a sip of water. Then he unbuttoned his top button as he started to feel the heat spread across his body.

"This doll dates to the disappearances of 1935—the child performers from the circus. It reappeared when I lost my niece fifteen years ago, when this Raggedy Ann doll belonged to her. And five days ago, I found another Raggedy Ann in the shrub where they tried to take the boy."

"Is this one of your paranormal tours, Digger? You expect us blokes to believe your bullshit story?" said one of the townsfolk, a younger man who was a newbie in town.

An older man, who appeared to be in his eighties, stood up, holding his walking stick. "Let me tell you something, young man; I was here when Digger lost his niece. It was the eeriest experience this town ever had. It rocked the foundations of this place, and many people left because of it. They'd had enough. It was the straw that broke the camel's back. And my father told me the stories of the lost circus performers and how those children mysteriously disappeared and were later found dead."

"Thank you, George, for yer comments. You have always been a good mate and cared for the welfare of our community," said Digger.

Another man dressed in farmer clothes with a pit bull tied on a leash stood up. "Listen here, mate; I have known you for a long time, and we have shared many beers together. Plenty of moments, good and bad. I want to say that I feel for what has happened, but we gotta let go—walk away from this curse that has swallowed our town. Those days are gone, and I don't want to hold on to those superstitions that our parents taught us while growing up anymore."

The room broke out into a spirited debate as the townsfolk split between those who wanted to continue with opening day and those who wanted to delay it. People stood up and pointed at each other as families sided with those with the same point of view. Clarisse could hardly hear herself think as she turned back toward Harry and raised her hand in the air, suggesting that she intervene. Harry shook his head, wanting her to stay out of the political debate and leave it for Digger to handle.

The debate was no longer a reasonable discussion between like-minded people with the same objectives. It deteriorated out of control as some older folks decided they'd had enough and commenced walking out. Then, out of the blue, Shamy stood up and pelted his cane against the wooden seat in front of him—*bang, bang*. The loud clap ricocheted off the walls and through eardrums.

Everyone stopped dead in their tracks and stood still, peering at him.

"I'm Shamy. Most of the people here know me, or at

least knew my father. Some of the older folks present would've known my grandpa." He looked around the room with an intense glare, his brown-black eyes looking right through people.

Most people avoided his gaze by looking down. They didn't necessarily like Shamy, but they respected him. He had authority and a mystique about him that many believed to have come from a line of shamans with supernatural powers.

"Some of you think the town is under a curse. You are all wrong. It's worse than that. Since 1935, this town has been under the influence of a demon and a band of loyal followers—the evil crew. Transient souls that have decided to make this town their own. For over a hundred years, this town went to sleep, and so did the evil with it. But now you have woken it up with the development of the pioneering village. The demon senses the opportunity to become stronger and spread its wings.

"My father and grandpa fought this demon while you all went about your normal lives. We protected you from its wrath in ways you will never understand, a legacy that I inherited from my father from a long line of Christian fighters of the faith."

Shamy raised his head high and looked toward Digger with the pride and spirit of a man full of admiration. "That man over there, our entrepreneur who has rebuilt this town, lost his niece to the same evil that has come back today." He paused for a moment to take a breath. "Digger is a proud man of Old Tailem Town, and he is also a skeptic sometimes, questioning everything mystical about this place. However, he is standing in front of you today, sharing his concern for the young children, and all you can do is yell at each other and throw insults?"

"But what about the girl?" asked Kezza abruptly. "It all started when *she* came to town, asking questions about the graveyard, the exhumed graves … She even went to Payneham to dig through the archives. She is nothing but trouble."

There was a murmur in the church as everyone turned to face Clarisse, staring with curiosity.

Clarisse turned red and looked down while she tapped her foot on the floor nervously.

"Now, now. That will be enough, Kezza," said Digger. Everyone in town knew how difficult Kezza was—raw, unsophisticated, and downright rude when she wanted to be.

"Since Clarisse has been in town, she has found out more about the evil than we could've. With her partner, Harry, and his investigative skills, they have taken it upon themselves to find the facts about what happened here, and all of this without anyone's help from us, me included."

Shamy took his seat, asking Digger to move on with the meeting now that they had made their point.

Jacko, the mechanic, raised his hand and yelled across the room, "I put forward a motion that opening day be delayed by a month to give us more time to sort this problem out. We need to give Shamy more time to do his work." He looked directly at Clarisse and said, "And what about you, luv? Will you be staying behind to support Shamy? We could do with your help."

"Yes, let's put it to a vote," said an old man at the back of the church.

Within moments, everyone supported Jacko's motion, and Digger acknowledged the action.

"Right-o then, this is the motion. Those of you who agree to postpone opening day by one month, raise yer hands."

A steady show of hands filled the room with a two-thirds majority.

"It looks like the ayes have it," confirmed Digger. "The motion is passed."

Kezza stood up angrily, red-faced, with sharp eyes and her nose scrunched up as she pointed at Digger. "Do you know what this is going to mean for my motel business!"

"I'm sorry, Kezza, but we are all going to be affected," said Digger.

"And what about my money? Do I get my investment back?" asked another man who happened to be one of the financiers.

"If we don't fix this problem, once and for all, and something happens on opening day, God forbid we lose another child. You can all kiss yer arses goodbye, because *no one* will come here to this town ever again. Old Tailem will become a ghost town once more. Is that what you blokes want?"

Kezza stormed out, along with another group of people, mainly financiers and new townsfolk who thought his whole "evil talk" was a typical small-town mentality. They would never buy into Shamy's explanation, too naïve and dismissive to even explore the circumstances. They shut the door on any possibility of a united front. They would go it alone, a breakaway group in the pioneering village.

Unaware to anyone, the demon watched while perched on the ceiling beam, out of sight. It licked its lips, the elongated forked red tongue slithering outward. Controversy, bickering, and feuding amongst the townsfolk was precisely the outcome it preyed upon, its mantra to conquer and divide. The demon couldn't help but grin as its saber-like yellow teeth protruded beyond its mouth in a show of despicable ugliness. But the demon kept its distance, knowing Shamy was in the room. It feared Shamy and his power, unable to break down its resistance for centuries now, and the demon knew its place.

As the townsfolk left the church, bickering amongst each other, the overcrowded sound of people rumbling was interrupted by a loud cry.

"We can't find Oliver! Hurry! Someone help!" It was the cry of a teenage boy standing in the graveyard next to the church.

The demon looked on from the ceiling of the church, realizing an opportunity. It quietly transitioned to the graveyard under the moonlight. He gave the order to his evil crew to attack the child.

Little Oliver hid behind a gravestone next to the outlying shrub, unaware that the demon lay waiting to pounce with all its magical trickery and deception.

"Come play with me. Come play with me." It was a Raggedy Ann doll peering from the shrub, calling out in a squeaky, puppet-like voice.

Little Oliver looked on, mesmerized, as he walked toward the doll.

The Raggedy Ann doll smiled, and its mouth moved, synchronized like a ventriloquist's doll. "Come play with me. Come play with me." The doll waved its little arms around and became more animated as little Oliver got closer.

Little Oliver's friend looked on as he ran toward him, thinking it was a game.

"Found you, found you. You're it!" he yelled across a row of graves behind little Oliver.

As little Oliver got within arm's length of the doll, the wind changed directions, and an icy breeze blew across the graveyard. The shrubs and eucalyptus trees swayed from the unexpected gust of wind as a putrid smell filled the air and a mist surrounded him to create camouflage.

Little Oliver screamed as the demon latched on to his ankles, piercing his skin with its devilish, elongated nails. Oliver was in pain as blood trickled down to his toes.

The demon dragged him into the shrub while little Oliver latched on to anything to hold his ground. Kicking and scraping the dirt, he managed to grab ahold of a low-lying branch big enough to act as an anchor point, but how long could an eight-year-old boy continue to fight against such immense power?

"Help, help!" he yelled, the screams heard as far as the church.

Digger took hold of his flashlight, followed by Jacko and Harry, as they all raced toward the graveyard to save the boy.

The townsfolk looked on from the gravel car park in horror as the events unfolded in front of them. Everything that Digger had warned them about was playing out like a reality TV show.

Shamy stayed behind in the church, grabbing Clarisse's arm when she was on her way to join them. "They are not going to be able to save him by fighting the demon on its turf. Follow me."

As soon as the church emptied, Shamy slammed the door shut then dashed toward the trapdoor, flinging it open in a mad rush.

"Come. I know you have been down here before," said Shamy.

Clarisse followed him down the stairs and into the crypt with her flashlight, shutting the trapdoor behind her. They didn't want to be seen by anyone, since it was a secret room.

"Listen here, luv; the demon has taken the boy's

physical body, but not his soul. There is a gap before that happens, but time's running out," said Shamy.

Clarisse looked on and nodded. She did not mutter a word as she watched the master shaman go to work.

He lifted the lid from the small chest holding the *carbonados*. "Do you know the prayer to the holy virgin mother?"

"Yes."

"Pray with me." Shamy placed his hand over the *carbonados* with an open palm and closed his eyes.

A light entered the crypt, magical, serene, and divine, spreading across the room. The energy was pure, innocent, spellbinding, and sturdy, radiating strength. She felt the presence of angels, although she could not see them.

Shamy was connected as he looked up and continued praying, tapping into the celestial energy, so immense it was apparent why demons felt hapless against it.

"The demon has taken him, but I know where to find the boy and bring him back. We need to act quickly."

"Where is the boy?" asked Clarisse. "I don't understand."

"We need to find the Raggedy Ann doll that lured him into the hands of the demon." Shamy closed the small chest then pointed to the trapdoor. "Come on, luv; we need to leave now and find Digger. He's out there, searching for him."

"Where can we find the doll?"

"It's in the shrub next to the graveyard. I had a vision. Let's get the bastard before it's too late."

Shamy was in his element, attacking the demon with all his power, experienced, knowing where to look. Clarisse didn't understand the source of his power, but that would have to wait for another time.

They raced to the graveyard, fighting time as the chances closed with every minute that passed by.

9 THE ROCKS

Digger had all the townsfolk willing to participate in a search line, approximately fifty yards long. Everyone carried a flashlight and a whistle. The children were told to follow behind their parents and bang on anything— pots, pans, timber, and even horns. They lined up outside the church where the graveyard met the shrub. The technique had been used many times in the past and had been introduced by the shaman. The idea was simple but effective. Demons did not like the limelight and being exposed, preferring to work in stealth, so they would run from advancing noise in fear of being found.

"Come on, you lot; let's flush the evil mongrel out," said Digger, pointing ahead into the darkness of the shrub. "Follow me and keep the line straight. Make noise and look for clues anywhere."

Jacko took the first line of attack. He was experienced and had done this before when Digger had lost his niece. On that day, they had searched hard and long through the dense shrub but had never found her. It had to do with timing. As Shamy had pointed out, the running was short. Miss that opportunity, and there was no way to bring your child back.

Shamy caught up to Digger and advised which direction to take. It was the shaman's responsibility to lead the way through his vision.

"The demon has taken the child to the rocks," said Shamy.

Digger looked at Shamy. "The locals are shit-scared of the rocks. Once they know we are going there, they will leave the search."

The rocks were a mystical place, drawn on superstition and the occult. More than a hundred years ago, a band of vagabonds and gypsies had settled there. They had been wizards and witches who had the local townsfolk spooked. Headless cows and decapitated chickens had been found next to rabbits hanging from tree branches. At night, the embers of their fires had filled the sky above the rocks, the ritualistic song and beating drums heard in the distance.

"No worries, mate. Not everyone in the line knows about the rocks. If we lose some of the old-timers on the way, that's fine—we have enough people."

Clarisse and Harry joined the search line behind Shamy. They felt an obligation to participate and find Oliver. They had no affinity with the rocks—neither spooked—and they were battle-hardened by demons from past encounters.

"All right, you lot, follow me toward the rocks. Keep the line straight and make as much noise as you can!" said Digger.

The line moved forward at a steady pace as the flashlights of approximately fifty people lit up the shrub in a display of shadow walkers. They scrummaged through broken branches, kicking them off the ground to find clues. The men smashed limbs off the low-lying trees to ensure nobody was hiding.

"Remember to look for clues!" shouted Shamy. He was not one for his vocal intensity; however, this situation demanded it. He was in his element, determined to track down the boy and save him from a life of darkness.

Suddenly, the line stopped at the blow of a horn. Someone had found the boy's shoe and buttons from his shirt.

"It belongs to little Oliver," said Shamy. "We are heading in the right direction."

"All right, listen up; we found Oliver's shoe. Follow me up to the rocks, hold that line steady, make noise.

Let's go!" Digger moved on as he led the search party closer to the demon's hideaway.

Shamy stopped dead in his tracks, sending a chain reaction throughout the search party. The banging stopped and everyone looked at him. Eyes shut, he concentrated while holding his cross with his left hand.

"What is it, mate?" asked Digger.

"Something's out there," he said

"I can feel it, too. It's Little Charlie." Clarisse had tapped into his energy.

"He's not the only one. There's more … a whole line of them."

The search party waited for instructions, standing with their flashlights pointing directly in front, but they could not see anything.

"Did you hear that? The giggle?" asked Clarisse. There was also a clatter of footsteps stepping on broken branches, twigs, and leaves ahead.

"The demon has sent the evil crew to slow us down. They are going to play all sorts of tricks to stop us." Shamy turned around toward the search party and said, "Don't be frightened. They are trying to scare us and slow us down, but they can't hurt you while I'm here."

"What's with the circus music I hear? There's no circus around here," said Digger.

"I can hear it, too." It was a familiar sound to Clarisse from her previous encounter in the graveyard.

"Ignore the circus music, everyone. Let's press on!" Shamy was in the mood to tackle the evil crew head-on.

"You heard the man." Digger was defiant, waving his hand in the air like a captain. "One straight line, keep making noise, and don't worry about the circus tune. Straight for the rocks ahead!"

Connected to the spirits, she caught glimpses of the evil crew. Little Charlie was hanging off a branch, waving as he tried to frighten the search party away. One of the girls flung herself from tree to tree like a trapeze act, and the other threw pieces of dead wood and branches on the ground at the feet of the advancing search team. Their strategy was creating an environment of fear, playing on the senses of the search party and hoping they would be spooked and run away. But they feared Shamy and his power and couldn't get close enough. It was like he was carrying a spiritual shield that protected everyone. The demon knew this, biding time. The longer he dragged this on, the closer he got to stealing the boy's soul.

"There are the rocks!" yelled Digger. "One last push. Hold the line, make noise, look for clues!"

They were less than twenty yards away from the rocks—boulders of ancient stone formation that was synonymous with the spiritual world. The perfect place for a demon to hide.

There was the sound of another horn. Someone had found something, a clue.

"What is it?" yelled Digger.

"A doll … Raggedy Ann!" one of the search party members called out. "But it's cut in half."

Digger looked at Shamy, seeking advice.

"Let's move onto the rocks and get the bastard!"

The banging became more intense as the search party reached the edge of the rock formation and the crevasse where they expected the demon to be holding the boy. It was a race against time, and they had to act quickly.

"Why is time so important?" asked Clarisse.

Shamy looked at her with a spiritual strength that she had never felt before. "I need you to be brave and come with me to confront the demon. Whatever you do, don't negotiate with it. And don't look into its eyes."

Clarisse nodded, sensing a skirmish.

"The demon is negotiating with his master to take the boy. It's like an assessment. If the master agrees, he will reward the demon with more privileges."

"Negotiating?" Clarisse was perplexed.

"Demons have a structure, a pecking order. They need to satisfy its master of evil, demonstrate their prowess."

"A type of review?"

"Yes, that's where the time comes into it. The demon master needs time to assess the situation, the test."

"Doesn't his master know we are on our way to confront it?"

"That's the whole point. They are watching to see if the demon is smart enough to rally his crew and turn us around."

"They are watching the whole thing develop?"

"Yes."

"And if he fails?"

"We get the boy back, and his master won't be happy with him."

"Will they remove his powers?"

"Not always. Sometimes, they don't have a replacement straight away." Shamy took hold of Clarisse's palm. "I need you to be strong and turn your spiritual energy on the demon."

Clarisse smiled. "I'm ready."

"Hold the line here, Digger. I'm going in with Clarisse."

Digger acknowledged his instructions and called the search party to a halt but to keep making noise.

Shamy and Clarisse left the group for the rocks,

stepping over the crushed stones and brittle wood that lay in their path.

At the crevasse, they saw little Oliver sitting on a rock, crying, begging for help. Frightened, he was asking for his mum and dad. It had been a harrowing ordeal for an eight-year-old.

Clarisse felt for him and wanted to help him straight away, but Shamy held on to her arm and asked her to stay.

"Crickey, he's baiting you with the boy," said Shamy. "This demon knows your weakness. Little Charlie would've told him everything about you."

"We can't stand by and watch!"

"Here, luv, hold this and follow me." It was a *carbonados* stone but smaller than the one in the crypt, a pocket-sized version that Shamy carried with him everywhere, tied around his neck with a leather chain.

It felt warm in her hand, alive, and made her feel safe, brimming with confidence.

They stepped onto the rocks and, only feet away from little Oliver, Shamy knelt in prayer and asked Clarisse to hold out the *carbonados*.

"Help me, help me. I wanna go home," Oliver cried and shook from the intense fear that occupied his young mind.

"Pray with me," said Shamy.

The demon, furious by their presence, circled indulgently, cockily, trying to intimidate as it sought to confront Shamy. The evil crew surrounded little Oliver to shield him.

They were so close, and time was running out. Clarisse wanted to let go and make a dash for little Oliver, not able to stand the boy's torment anymore.

The demon with his angular face circled them. Red, bloodshot eyes and a slimy, forked tongue elongated like a hissing lizard, staring directly toward them intimidatingly. His feet had transformed into the hooves of a bull with a curled-up tail and hairy legs as he threw a temper tantrum by crushing rocks with every kick.

A putrid, gaseous smell filled the air, and Clarisse had to place her hands over her mouth and nose, unprepared for the stench, though she should have known better.

Behind the demon, his evil crew were at work, forming a circle around little Oliver. They stood there, one yard apart, arms crossed, except for Little Charlie, who took a spot on the rock above them, looking outwardly. Too immature to receive any instructions, they used him as a lookout. Happy to play with his rope, he enjoyed the show.

The demon circled, and Shamy kept pushing him

back with his energy and prayers. Then came the time to act. He turned to Clarisse and said, "When I say go, get the boy as quickly as you can and bring him to me."

Clarisse nodded and waited.

Shamy took the *carbonados* from Clarisse then launched it in front of him with two hands outstretched. "I repel you, demon! Go forth and leave this place!"

Radiant energy materialized, thrusting the demon into the air and onto the rocks. It was an energy source so powerful that the evil crew were blindsided and defenseless.

"Go now!"

Clarisse ran toward little Oliver and grabbed the boy from the circle of evil, unbeknownst to the evil crew as the energy engulfed them.

Clarisse held him tightly as he sobbed over her shoulder. "I want my mummy and daddy," he cried profusely with tears of pain and happiness that he was out of the demon's clasp.

Shamy grabbed them both by a shoulder and escorted them from the rocks and to the safety of Digger and the search party.

"Don't look back!" he said. The *carbonados* stone did not have infinite energy, and it would only last a short while, just long enough to get them to safety.

Soon, Oliver was in the arms of his mother and father. They hugged and kissed, grateful for the return of their boy.

Shamy knew the parents. They were locals who had lived in the area for generations. It made the ordeal more emotional for him because they had grown up in a small community. Getting back little Oliver was always going to be a personal thing.

Shamy went over to Clarisse to thank her for her strength and support.

"You're one hell of a spirit fighter, luv, but it's not over," said Shamy

"What do you mean? Haven't we beaten it?"

"No, luv, he will come back at us, more determined than before, like a mongrel dog. We made him look bad in front of his master."

"Like a final battle? Stronger, you mean?"

"Yeah, because if he fails again, his master will send him back to the inferno to a life of living hell. That lot don't take any prisoners."

"Fire and brimstone?"

Shamy nodded. "We need to be ready for the next fight. It could happen at any time. And if I was a demon, what better way than to wreak havoc on opening day."

"We haven't checked the storage room in the church

yet." Clarisse crossed her arms and blinked a few times, starting to get tired.

"Ah, yeah. Raggedy Ann, the evil's conduit. Let's do that tomorrow in the arvo."

The next day, Digger offered Clarisse a ride to the church in Old Tailem Town. It suited him because he had to prepare for a booked-out series of paranormal tours in the evening.

"Looks like Kezza and her financiers got the lawyers onto us," said Digger. It angered him as he let go his frustration on his car, thrashing the engine on the way to Old Tailem Town.

"Does that mean you can't stop opening day?"

"Yep. The whole thing has to do with the contract, and my lawyer said I have no hope of defending it. Crickey, he said I couldn't stop a public event because of some supernatural stuff."

"They must think we are a pack of crackpots."

Digger looked across to Clarisse with a sarcastic grin as he made fun of Kezza by imitating her voice. "Yeah, and Shamy is a lunatic living in la-la land."

Clarisse laughed. "That's a really good impersonation."

"I know that woman like the back of my hand;

imitating her is easy."

"What about your paranormal tours—the main attraction? Are you going to continue with your shows on opening day?"

"The letter from her lawyers says if I don't run my paranormal tours, they will sue me for damages. I feel like fighting that angry woman, but I don't have the sort of money for lawyers—Kezza is the richest woman in town, you know." He parked the car by applying the brakes heavily, making it skid to a stop on the gravel. "I reckon I have a couple of ideas up my sleeve that will help us on opening day. We can talk about that later on, luv."

Clarisse thanked him for the ride then checked the time on her cell phone.

Yep, three p.m., as planned and right on time, she thought.

Once inside the church, she looked around for Shamy, but he was uncharacteristically late.

It was serene and quiet as the sunlight filtered through the stained glass, creating a mosaic effect. Bands of shaded yellow, green, and blue interloped each other, causing a luminance across the hall. The allure was nebulous, as though someone had cast a magic spell.

She sat in the front row behind the altar, floating into a daydreamer's gaze and closing her eyes. Many thoughts transpired from her mind, none other than her latest experience with little Oliver and the demon.

She felt a tap on her right shoulder, like the tip of a finger with longish nails. She shrugged as a tickling sensation progressed down her back, causing her posture to pull upright. She hesitated. Something was in the room and behind her.

Impulsively, she wanted to turn around to see what it was; however, instinct told her to keep looking ahead with her eyes fixated on the statue of Jesus.

Another tap on her left shoulder, more pronounced, made her shrug her shoulders even more. It was no longer a coincidence or a thing of nature. The touch felt devoid of any life—cold and unappealing.

That's it, she thought.

She turned her head valiantly to find the demon sitting two rows back.

"Don't mean to startle you, miss. I have a distorted face. Hit a bus before I died and can't do much about it now." His angular face, broken nose, lack of ears, and the stitches running along the side of his face made his despicable presence unpleasurable.

"How did you tap me from over there? Surely, your arms don't reach that far."

The demon laughed and said, "I'm a demon and can

touch you from any distance. I don't need to be sitting next to you."

"What do you want, demon? I know you're not talking to me for the fun of it." She turned around, gazing directly at the evil. She didn't fear demons anymore, and that was the reason Shamy had called upon her to assist with the flashbacks.

"You are an impatient mortal. Let me cut to the chase and tell you what's on my mind." The demon paused then levitated off the chair in an exhibit of mighty power before settling on a church beam ahead. Looking down below, he continued. "Miss, the master thinks I was not generous enough the first time we met, and we have an opportunity for you."

Clarisse did not react to the demon's con words. "You can't trick me. You should know that about me by now."

"This is not a trick but an opportunity. Hear me out. I can offer you more power than you could imagine. A guarantee you don't need to satisfy anyone from the underworld—a standalone position with a level of authority and one legion of demons at your command. That's a hell of a lot more than I have; excuse the pun."

"And that does not come for free." Clarisse's felt a pinch in her outstretched neck muscles as she looked toward the ceiling.

"There is a little something we need to complete our offer."

"And what may that be?"

"That black stone in the crypt."

"No way, demon. You want me to give up the power of the *carbonados*, the only force capable of repelling you and your evil crew?"

"Well, miss, you wouldn't be the first one to jump ship for eternal pleasure unbound in this world." The demon laughed, and it reverberated throughout the church hall. "Or you can live your life like the shaman— alone on a farm, drinking tea all day and praying to your Lord above for forgiveness. Boring, if you ask me."

"You want the *carbonados* that badly?"

"We all want and need something badly in life. It depends on what it is."

Clarisse could not understand what the demon was leading to but, in her experience, she had learned they liked talking in riddles. It was their way of toying with you until they got straight to point.

"And, miss, how forgetful of me. There is one other offer I would like to make."

Clarisse rubbed her neck to help relieve the muscle strain.

"If you agree to our terms, I will return the soul of Digger's niece to him. There is not much I can do with her physical body fifteen years later, but I will free her from my control and hand her soul back. Call it an exchange." The demon swung from one beam to another, causing Clarisse to change her posture. "As for you, miss, I will give you back the soul of Little Charlie, so he can leave this transient state and make his way to your Lord and join his departed family. And yeah, I know how obsessed you have become with the cuddly boy. Ha, ha. So, what do you say?"

Clarisse sat motionless, lost for words as she placed her hands over her face, saddened and teary-eyed.

"You have until tomorrow." The demon vanished, leaving Clarisse with a painful decision that affected the souls of both Little Charlie and Digger's niece. She was tormented further by her responsibility for the souls of countless children who would be exposed to this malingering evil on opening day.

She felt an enormous burden placed on her shoulders. But that was the devil's game—a shrewd negotiator, knowing when to strike. Playing on the fears and emotions of mortals, a weakness he did not have to endure in the hellish world of demons.

As for opening day, another human frailty—conquer

and divide. Oh yes, the demon could always rely on greed to run its course and split the community, despite the inherent dangers. And let's not forget the shaman, a man who could defend the town when needed but never made it his mission to seek and destroy the evil, even though he had immense power at his disposal.

Another human conditioning was preferring to let sleeping dogs lie. Old Tailem Town had lost its fear, and the demon had sensed it. The townsfolk maintained an attitude of appeasement rather than a determination to cleanse the town. It was what kept the devil and his evil crew hanging around, waiting for their moment.

10 RAGGEDY ANN

Clarisse continued to sit in the church, waiting for Shamy, pondering her duel with the demon. The thought would not go away as she faced a personal dilemma.

She heard the jolt of the main door opening then felt a gust of air rush through the air. It was a blustery day in Old Tailem with a north wind powering down the main street, lifting dust in its wake.

"Caught ya at a bad time, luv? You look pissed off," said Shamy. "You look like you have lots on your mind, too." Shamy could sense something wrong, as he could see through people's emotions.

Clarisse turned around and asked him to take a seat. "There is something I want to ask you."

"Okay, shoot; tell me what's on your mind."

"I don't understand why you have not confronted the demon after all this time. Your family has been here for over a hundred years."

"You mean, get rid of it once and for all?"

"Well, you have the power, don't you? I can see it fears you."

He crossed his legs and clasped his ancient book with both hands. "My father always said it was better to manage the demon than have an all-out war. Evil is everywhere, and as soon as you get rid of one, another takes its place. It's a never-ending cycle."

"Well, it continues to mock us and divide our community; can't you see that?"

"I understand what ya are saying, and I am living with that thought all the time.

"Going back to the Byzantine period, my ancestors would rage battle on demons with the black stone—the *carbonados*. It was a constant and never-ending battle for supremacy. I reckon they lost many priests in the process. Eventually, the Order of the Sepaline settled for containment, preferring to manage the demons, to keep an eye on them, intervening only when it got out of hand."

"What's the Order of the Sepaline?" Clarisse's forehead crinkled as she gazed directly at him with a sharp-eyed focus.

"I will explain it to you one day, luv, but not today. It's a long story."

"How have you *managed* this demon? He mocks you, ignores you. It will unleash on opening day while the town is full of children."

Shamy stood silent and didn't react.

"Do you ever get concerned it may be taking advantage of your containment approach? It keeps pushing the boundaries each time, checking to see how strong you are. It splinters your powers. It has become smarter, and it plays off our greed by dividing the town." Clarisse was letting it all out, her emotions running high.

"Bloody oath, all those points ya make are true. It's okay to get those things off your chest; I'm not offended. And crikey, what I like about ya is you speak your mind." Shamy took hold of Clarisse's arm. "You think I have never doubted myself about the way I manage the demon? Come on, luv; we have a job to do now—find that Raggedy Ann and destroy it."

Clarisse nodded, wiping a tear from her eye with her index finger. She had been through an emotional roller coaster and was still learning to cope with the situation.

They walked to the back of the church, behind the vestry, to a small, ominous door that was bolted with a padlock that must have been part of the original church.

"I haven't been here for over fifteen years; never needed to go looking for anything. We talked about clearing it out many years ago, but nobody wanted to take responsibility for it." Shamy had a chain full of keys, yet he had forgotten which was the right one. Eventually, after the tenth attempt, he managed to unlock the mortise padlock and pushed the jammed door open with both hands.

It was a dusty, dark, dreary room with no light switch, designed like a walk-in closet with barely enough room for two people. Cardboard and wooden boxes lay on top of each other, thrown about without a care or in any logical order.

"This place is a pigsty full of dead bugs and cockroaches," said Shamy.

Clarisse coughed and waved her hands as a breeze blew in through the front entrance, penetrating the storage room and lifting an inch of dust into the air.

"We should remove the boxes one by one into the light so we can check inside."

It was not the first time Clarisse had to inspect old boxes. During her visit to Hartley Town, she had spent days sifting through old boxes in the cellar underneath the presbytery. She liked snooping through historical notes and artifacts, looking for clues. It was something she had learned from Harry.

She waited for the dust to settle, a glittering haze that

mixed with the light filtering through the church window. Then, as she removed the first box from the top pile, she heard a rattle, like something was bouncing around inside a box on the lower shelf.

"Have we got mice in here?" she asked.

Shamy looked inside to inspect the noise, but it was gone.

She continued lifting the box from the rack, placing it on the floor outside the room, when she heard the same rattle again.

"This time I heard it!" said Shamy.

They both looked inside the storage room, and the sound of the rattling became more pronounced.

"Look, it's coming from that wooden box on the middle shelf over there." Clarisse pointed to an old-style, timber-constructed box that had been used in the days when there was no cardboard for storage.

Each time they stepped into the storeroom, there was the rattle, sensing their presence. Something was in the box, and it wasn't mice, as there were no holes in the compartment that was sealed with thick rope. Then came a stench from the same container. It was a gaseous smell, putrid, but it only lasted for a short while.

How could that be? she thought. Something was toying with them, a warning.

"You hold on to the box while I cut the rope," said Shamy. He was not intimidated by its presence. Why should he? After all, he was the shaman.

Clarisse picked up the wooden box of medium size and close to the dimensions of an archive box. It rattled with furor and intent as whatever was inside felt like it was being suspended off the steady racking. She struggled to maintain her balance as the rattling became more intense.

Shamy grabbed the side of the box in anticipation to support her. Another whiff of stench came from it, but this time sharper, more vulgar at best, and distinct. She felt a burning sensation on her fingertips rise through to her hands as she gripped the box reluctantly, wanting to let go.

"Should we open it?" she asked.

"No, that's what the bloody thing wants. Run and open the trapdoor to the crypt, luv. I'm taking it there."

Clarisse let go of the box then dashed to the trapdoor at the rear of the church. She lifted the door then switched on the solitary light.

"It's open!" she yelled out. "It's open!"

Shamy could not see her from the storage room since the altar was blocking his view.

He held the box firmly as the rattling became

intense, making it difficult for him to maintain a solid grip and balance as he steadily walked toward the entrance of the crypt. Whatever was inside the box sensed the power of the *carbonados.*

With every yard traveled, the rattling and a burning sensation in his hands started to affect his grip. There was a limit to the pain that he could endure.

The burning sensation became unbearable as his fingers started to feel the pinch of heat, and the gaseous smell made him hold his breath intermittently. He felt like vomiting.

As he got to the trapdoor and took his first step down the staircase and into the crypt, a sharp impulse pierced through his hand, making his muscles and nerves fail. He had to let go, or he would go crashing down onto the stone floor.

The box tumbled down the staircase, rolling over and over as it gained momentum before crashing onto the stone floor and ricocheting off the wall. The top of the box broke off the damaged frame, and wooden fragments were thrown across the room, splinters pointing in every direction like small javelins.

Clarisse threw her arms in front of her to protect herself from the flying debris.

And there it was, standing in the corner of the

room—the same Raggedy Ann doll that Shamy remembered from when he had been a child, still in Old Tailem Town, spreading its evil. The devil's concubine, responsible for luring children to a dark fate.

Every devil had a tool of the trade, an inconspicuous piece. There was no limit to the ingenuity of what a demon could use to lure its prey, like a mousetrap.

The doll with its curly red hair and green and white clothes stood upright, grinding its teeth. Only its mouth could move; nothing else. Nevertheless, it made no sound.

"The *carbonados*!" yelled Shamy. "Open the black box!" He was on the other side of the room, the Raggedy Ann standing between them.

Clarisse looked toward the black box, took one deep lunge, and threw herself onto the table. Energy was filtering out from the black box, holding the Raggedy Ann at bay as it continued grinding its teeth.

She lifted the black box's lid, and the splendor of the *carbonados* black stone lit up with an intensity that filled the room.

Shamy broke out into a Byzantine prayer, sensing the Raggedy Ann was facing its execution from the protectorate—a long line of departed priests who had carried the same powers of the shaman centuries ago.

The Raggedy Ann stopped grinding then caught fire.

Clarisse covered her eyes at the intense blinding light and heat that filled the room. There were no remnants, not even a smell. The doll simply vaporized, as though it had never existed. The devil's tool and concubine was gone, defeated.

Clarisse sat on the staircase and took a deep breath. She looked toward Shamy, who continued praying, kneeling at the altar and next to the black box.

"Do you think you might be able to explain all this to me?" She crossed her arms over her chest. "I mean, how did you vaporize the Raggedy Ann? And the *carbonados*; where did that stone come from?"

Shamy completed his prayer then made the sign of the cross before he stood up and told Clarisse they had to leave now. He was exhausted from the doll's exorcism.

"I will explain everything to you in good time, luv. But now is not the right moment."

"Then explain to me how you vaporized the Raggedy Ann. Tell me that." Clarisse was persistent and emotional.

"The power in the stone and my prayer exorcised it."

"You exorcised a doll? It can't be—it has no soul. It's not a living thing."

"That is a myth. For God's sake, a demon can take possession of an object with no soul and plant its evil seed. It can be the soul of an evil entity it captured a long time ago and found some use for."

"So, it could take over a mirror, a chair … practically anything it finds useful and manifest itself through that object, as a tool or conduit?"

"Correct. They don't have the same rules as you and I, the same barriers and beliefs." Shamy stood up and closed the black box gently before wiping the dust off with his black robe. "If you want to defeat a demon, you need to think like one, not see the world in a two-dimensional way like most people."

"But you have been taught that way. Generations of shaman, handed down from a young age. Us mere mortals could never understand."

"One day, when I feel you're ready, I will explain it to you. For now, our job is not done. We have opening day to contend with. I'm assuming Digger told you about the breakaway group?"

Clarisse nodded. "And I guess the demon knows opening day is going ahead."

"Oh, he knows. He probably planted the whole thing himself to divide the town. The demon has its sympathizers to help it do its work. You wouldn't know who they are because they master the cloak of disguise."

Digger arranged to drive Clarisse back to the motel. He waited at the front of the church in his car, peering through his driver's side window, smoking a cigarette. He had finished making some improvements to his paranormal tours, adding a new location to the itinerary. The recently renovated Ironmaker Workshop was known for the ghostly sightings of an old ironworker clamping away hot iron. An ominous figure of a man with a long, white beard and an eyepatch. Although Digger would say that he had heard about the legendary ghost from stories, he had never sighted it.

Clarisse exited through the church from the side entrance adjoining the graveyard to meet Digger.

"G'day, luv. Over here." He waved from the car then threw his cigarette butt on the gravel.

Clarisse stepped into the passenger seat and thanked him for the ride.

"You look out of sorts. Are ya all right?" he asked.

"Yeah, meditating and praying with Shamy can be draining, hard work." She kept the Raggedy Ann doll to herself. "I do want to ask you something …"

"Yeah, shoot; what's on yer mind?"

"Opening day is in four days; how are we going to protect the families?"

Digger paused for a moment to think about his

response. "I can't stop opening day from going ahead, but I am in charge of security. I have asked for help from my contacts in Payneham, a couple of retired policemen I've known for a long time. They are going to help out."

"Is that going to stop the evil crew from snatching children? I mean, we can't exactly see them."

Digger had a glitter in his eye. His entrepreneurial thinking had gone into overdrive. "Aha, but guess what, luv? What I do with the paranormal tour is my business, so I have called in some experts, added a new dimension to the show."

"What do you mean?"

"I hired these guys from the big smoke who do the paranormal ghost sightings. They have all this equipment, such as infrared, sound detectors … We will set up around the graveyard where most of the paranormal kidnappings occur."

Clarisse grinned. "That's pretty smart."

"Well, no one will know that I have set up an early detection system." He chuckled and smiled while looking directly at the road. "If our demon friend and his evil crew make any attempts to take a child, we will be onto it."

"That's very ingenious. Always coming up with the ideas. What would this town do without you?"

He acknowledged Clarisse's accolade with a smile.

Clarisse still had a lot on her mind, thinking about how the demon had offered her a deal that would deliver back Digger's niece's soul. She knew how much that girl had meant to him and the heartache her disappearance had caused. Bringing her back, her soul would cleanse all the pain Digger had endured for the past fifteen years. And as for Little Charlie, a devil that Clarisse had become fond of, she could release his soul from the demon, help him leave his transient state.

She had made plans to meet Shamy the next day to discuss another option for opening day. He had an idea, although a risky one, and wanted to ponder it overnight. Clarisse wasn't sure what was on his mind, but knowing Shamy, it could involve another flashback, but more intense.

Upon arriving at the Old Tailem Motel, Clarisse noted a small gathering of people near the front entrance. It was Kezza and her financiers, and they appeared to be in discussion, probably about opening day.

Digger predictably slammed on the brakes on the gravel road, finishing off with a skid and a plume of dust blowing toward them. They were annoyed, but they knew what Digger was like, so they simply shook their heads and dusted off their clothes.

"Looks like our mates are up to no good again," said Digger.

Clarisse thanked him for the ride then made her way to the entrance, bypassing Kezza and her financiers, the same people who were at the town hall meeting the other day. They occupied the whole entry, unperturbed that other patrons would also like to utilize the space to get in and out of the motel.

Kezza turned toward Clarisse in slow motion. Uncannily, her dark, red eyes flickered with a stealthy glare. "You should accept his offer, you know," she said.

Though she was speaking in slow motion, Clarisse managed to understand the words and was astonished. How would Kezza know about her encounter with the demon today at Old Tailem Church?

Kezza then turned around and continued her focus on the financiers. For a moment, it appeared that something had possessed Kezza to communicate with Clarisse, to remind her of the decision she had to make. She was in a dilemma.

Clarisse was having dinner with Harry in the motel restaurant. They hadn't seen each other much in the last few days with Harry working tirelessly on preparing the communication infrastructure in time for opening day.

He promised her that he would be done by the next day since they were in the final testing phase.

"You won't believe what I dug up in the archives today," said Harry.

"What do you mean? Weren't you working?"

"I had to go to Payneham to get some parts, and I had some downtime." Harry gave a childish grin, as though he had something up his sleeve.

"I've seen that look on you before. What is it?"

"The lady at the archive office … Maria? I think the more you see her, the more friendly she becomes. She gave me a clue that got me thinking."

"Come on; you've got me in suspense."

Harry opened his satchel and pulled out a police investigation report, placing it on the table. "Let me summarize this for you, as there's a lot to digest. At the time when the children went missing from the circus, the police were on the trail of this man who they suspected. He wasn't a local but worked his way through properties as a farmhand."

Clarisse knew who he was talking about, but asked anyway, "Are there any details on this man?"

"No names, only a description that's well defined." Harry sifted through the ten-page report to find the section. "Here it is. Have a read." He gently pushed the story toward Clarisse and pointed at the part of the page that contained the description.

> *A man in his thirties with a limp. He has a distinctive, pointed nose and angular face that protrudes from his flattened forehead. He was seen wearing a checkered shirt, straight-leg jeans with a rip down the side, and work boots with worn-out soles. He has a floral, red gypsy headband tied around his forehead and studded gold earrings. Drives a red pickup truck.*

> *He was last seen two days ago, drinking in the pub. The same day the children were listed as missing.*

Clarisse sat frozen, scratching her head, heart palpitating and legs shaking underneath the table.

"I have seen him before," admitted Clarisse, "in a flashback, a vision."

"How can that be? Probably a coincidence."

"No, I promise to God, it's the man in my vision."

Harry didn't know what to say, dumbstruck. He picked up the report and put it back in his pouch without muttering a word.

"Why is it you never believe me? Always thinking I'm making things up."

"I never said a word to you, Clarisse." He put his hand on her shoulder and looked her in the eye with a puppy dog look. "I'm still getting used to your paranormal stuff. I know you can see things that other people can't. I guess I'm still coming to terms with it."

"I'm visiting Shamy tomorrow. Do you mind if I show him the police report?"

"It's fine. I will leave it on the desk in our room. I'm shooting through early in the morning." Harry took a sip of wine then raised his head as though he wanted to say something but didn't.

"What is it?"

"There is one other thing I found, but I am not sure how relevant it is."

"Go on; tell me." Clarisse gave her total focus to Harry.

"I went through the gravesite manifest again and checked every grave record. Guess what I found."

She did not mutter a word, just looked at Harry with her almond-shaped, dark-brown eyes.

"I found an unmarked grave recorded at the time of the disappearance of Digger's niece."

"What are you saying—"

"I am not saying anything," Harry interrupted. "Probably a coincidence. But for what it's worth, the timing matches." Harry took another sip of wine. "Nobody died in Old Tailem for twelve months beforehand. I got a copy of the death registration."

"Harry, you are a sleuth. Totally in the wrong business." Clarisse shifted in her chair and filled her glass with the same white wine. "I can ask Shamy if he knows anything about the unmarked grave tomorrow."

He smiled and nodded. "Oh, leave it. The locals think we are digging our noses into everything. It was only for your information. Probably nothing."

Clarisse wanted to speak to Harry about her encounter with the demon in the church. However, she decided to leave it for another day.

He may poke fun at me, she thought.

For the first time since she had arrived in Old Tailem Town, Clarisse felt like she was homing in on the dark secrets that abounded in this place. Through a series of spiritual interventions and Harry's detective work, they were beginning to connect the dots.

She was sure about one thing: the demon and its evil crew were going to make a stand on opening day, a collision between good and evil. They had little time to build their spiritual defenses. To do that, they needed more information and, like Shamy said, *you need to think like the demon*. A lot depended on Shamy and his powers, and particularly how he was going to use them.

11 A DROPLET IN THYME

It was evening, and the dark-gray clouds hovered above, ready to shed their load of rain. The wind had shifted from a mild breeze to a burst of cold air as the weather front made its way through Old Tailem Town. Standing in the graveyard was dark and eerie this time of day, with the town empty of any human activity. It was a picture-perfect ghost town.

The only solitary streetlamp, leaning to one side, needed repair. It swayed in front of the church, barely making an impact, other than confirming the electricity grid was connected.

Improperly dressed for the elements, Clarisse shivered from the cold gusts. A light cotton cardigan was never going to be enough to keep her warm.

Before she could work out what she was doing there, the demon and his evil crew surrounded her. This was not like any other encounter. From the looks on their faces, they meant business.

The demon with the broken nose and angular face all stitched up nodded to his evil crew. It was time for the game of terror to begin.

Clarisse stood, an uncontrollable tremble filtering throughout her body. Her heart raced so fast that she could hear the pulse rebounding in her chest. She clasped both hands into fists as she waited for the first strike.

The girl in the crimson dress and black ponytail swung a hula hoop toward her, catching her perfectly as it slid down to her hips. Then another one hurtled toward her, more perfect than the first. It slid without touching her until it rested above the first hula, immobilizing her as she vigorously tried to remove it with no luck.

Then it was Little Charlie's turn as he swung his rope above his head then threw the lasso around Clarisse's neck. Clarisse grabbed the rope in fear she would choke to death and pulled on it with both hands, leaving a two-finger space between the lasso and her throat so she could breathe. But Little Charlie had no concept of pain and thought it was a game, so he threw another rope, the second falling over her head again, a perfect throw for a boy.

With hula hoops around her hips and two ropes around her neck, she felt hamstrung. Then the third child with the devilish red eyes and blood-stained dress—Clarisse remembered her as being the most potent of the lot—blew large bubbles the size of soccer balls that burst above her. Each burst resulted in a plume of gaseous smell that was so putrid it caused her to cough profusely, making it hard to hold her breath. It was the same stench she had encountered inside the church—an oxidizing fuel and chlorate combined.

"Your shaman can't help you now. Where is he with all his mighty powers from your God above?" said the demon, his arms crossed, grinning with fire in his eyes. He was enjoying every moment as the evil crew clapped in appreciation and continued their romp.

Clarisse felt a tug from the rope and fell to the ground, onto her back. Pulled by the hair, the pain was so intense she nearly fainted as the sensation ripped along her back and down to her legs. With her hand still between the rope and her neck, Little Charlie tugged her, scraping her along the ground covered in leaves, dried grass, and some gravel that pierced into her skin, scratching her back as her cardigan shredded.

After being yanked two yards, she felt drawn into a hole in the ground—a grave, waiting for her to be buried alive. She screamed so loud that she forgot about the stench, but no one could hear her, alone and at the fate of the demon.

"What do you want, demon?" she screamed.

"Nothing from you. This is a gift for my master. I'm sure he's enjoying every moment." The demon laughed, and it echoed into the distance, carried by a gust of wind.

The demon looked toward his evil crew and said, "Cover her up until I can't see her face anymore."

Clarisse screamed again. She didn't want to be buried alive. "Shamy, Harry, Digger ... where are you? Help me!"

She spat out the first handful of soil thrown into her face. Then another pail of dirt landed on her abdomen.

Clarisse screamed again, more frantically. It was her worst nightmare ... or was it even happening?

Little Charlie's face appeared above her at the top of the grave. He threw a rope and waved at her to come up while holding both hands in a locking grip. He signaled her to tug, trying to pull her out of the grave, in defiance of the demon's orders.

The demon felt angered and ridiculed by Little Charlie's rebellious streak. His master was watching, and all he could see was the demon's lack of control over his evil crew.

In a spat of anger, the demon took hold of Little Charlie's rope, wrapped it around him and flung him into the air.

Little Charlie's attempt to pull Clarisse out of the grave had failed. She was going to be buried alive.

More dirt was tossed onto her, pails and pails of it as it began to cover her head. Only her nose and eyes were left, peering above the soil line. She could not scream anymore, injured and paralyzed from head to toe. She could not breathe and started to choke as her lungs emptied of air. Was it the end?

Clarisse woke up from her nightmare, sweating all over and breathing deeply, gasping for air. She placed her hand on her chest to feel her heartbeat and measure her pulse. She looked around. She was at the motel, and she was alone. Harry must have slipped out to work early in the morning.

It had been a dream, but her dreams could also be a warning of things to come. She had learned to rely on them. She was ill at ease and worried something terrible was going to happen.

Clarisse had promised Shamy to be on time for their morning tea, but she was running late.

Clarisse managed to get ready as quickly as she could, cutting some corners with her makeup. She was a girl who always liked to look her best, but today, she would have to do without the intricate details.

She got ready in record time then dashed out to the waiting car, where Digger was on time, appearing calm as he smoked a cigarette while leaning against the driver's side door.

"You're late, but don't worry; I know how to make up time. We will cut through a dirt road," said Digger.

Clarisse was puffing as she jumped into the passenger seat, pleased to be underway. She didn't want to upset the shaman.

Shamy thought the setting of the old shed would be more appropriate for his next objective. The pure incense, harmony, and connection with God, which was out of bounds with demons could not infiltrate this place.

He was preparing something different that carried risk and would challenge whether Clarisse would be up for it. It was a spiritual ritual that could only be performed by experienced shamans. It needed two people to join, ready to pull one back should either of them encounter a problem. What awaited on the other side was the unknown, so it could go smoothly or badly. Many shamans had been lost using this technique through the ages, and so it was used less frequently, only by the approval of a high priest. However, Shamy felt he was getting to a point where he had limited options with a demon that was becoming virulent and growing in strength every day, on a quest to impress its master.

Opening day at the Pioneer Ghost Town of Old Tailem Town was heading toward a showdown, a battle between the powers of good and evil. It was all coming to a head within a divided town, as the demon purged its influence among the local sympathizers.

In many ways, the townsfolk were responsible for this undoing—a sleepy hallow turned upside down by entrepreneurs and financiers wanting to reap profit from the town's history. And while it was a quiet place, the demon had nothing to do in a ghost town outpost that had no life. It kept the devil sedated knowing it had nothing to strive for other than play-out time, waiting for something to happen.

Clarisse knocked on the door of the shed, arriving a few minutes late but not long enough to cause Shamy any concerns.

"How are you, luv? You look like you had a rough night. Did you get any sleep?"

Clarisse stepped inside and threw her bag on the antique wooden chair. "Can you tell I had a sleepless night?"

Shamy nodded as he sat down next to her. He looked

at her without saying much, sensing she had a lot on her mind. "The dark circles under your eyes are a dead giveaway."

"Ugh …" Clarisse smiled. "I want to talk to you about something. It's been keeping me up at night." She turned and looked at Shamy reluctantly, knowing she had to unleash on someone she could trust. "The demon tried to broker a deal with me."

Shamy jolted, lifting his head. "What type of deal?"

"The demon said he would give me all the powers and riches I could imagine."

"Is that it?"

"And release the spirits of Little Charlie and Digger's niece if I destroy the *carbonados*."

Shamy sighed. "Ugh, it's not the first time he's tried that trick." He shifted in his chair and crossed his legs while adjusting his black robe. "He attempted to con my father into a deal, although the demon was of a different appearance back then."

Clarisse was relieved that she was not alone and not the sole recipient of the demon's manipulative offer.

"What do I do? I could give Digger back the soul of his niece and release Little Charlie from his meaningless spiritual existence."

"Well, the demon is lying to you, luv. He is a

conman, a cheat, a manipulator. He can't release their souls, even if he wanted to. He doesn't have the power. Only his master can do that."

"So, how do I release their souls from a life of purgatory?"

"Crikey, sometimes you can't. They remain stuck for centuries until they negotiate their way out. The only other way is to defeat the bastards so they can break away from their hold."

Shamy had a hot brew of local tea on the side table and offered Clarisse a cup. She took a sip then sat back in the chair as the frankincense started to take effect. Relaxed and peaceful, she was finding solace.

"So, the same demon tried to make a deal with your father?" asked Clarisse.

"Yeah, same demon but different appearance, luv. They are shifters, continuously altering their image so they can stay undetected. When you go through events dating back to 1935, you will find other people coming and going. It's the same demon, so don't be fooled."

"I wanted to ask you about the graveyard … you know … the unmarked graves."

"You're interested in who's buried in those graves?"

Clarisse nodded and put the cup of tea on the table.

"You had a dream, didn't you?" Shamy picked up his

leather-bound book from the table and held it with both hands. "They tried to bury you alive?"

Clarisse was stunned by the revelation. *How does he know about that?*

"This demon is powerful and can poke your mind when you are sleeping, fill you with warnings and thoughts of horror to throw you off guard." Shamy was not mincing words.

She leaned forward, silenced by the disclosure.

"As for who is in those unmarked graves, who knows? There are lots of theories floating around, but no one's dared to unearth them. Superstition, you know."

Clarisse needed time to ponder his points of view. There was a lot of information trading hands, and she needed to manage her thoughts.

"Let's go for a walk in the herb garden," Shamy said, sensing the overload information dump. They both needed a time-out to recalibrate their focus.

The herb garden was manicured, organized, and had everything one could imagine, a chef's paradise. The fragrance from the rosemary, parsley, thyme, and other herbs all mixed to make a cacophony of scents that were truly calming and cleansing on the soul. It was understandable why Shamy spent so many hours cultivating his garden, disconnected from the rest of the world. Clarisse thought this would be an excellent opportunity to understand his hermit ways, the isolation from the rest of the community.

"I wanted to ask why the townsfolk consider you a recluse. I can see you spend a lot of time in your garden."

"Is this an interview, luv?"

She stopped, turned toward Shamy, and looked directly into his eyes. "No, I want to know and understand the way you think, spiritually."

He paused for a moment and thought about his words. "It's inner silence, a sense of deep stillness. I think most people underestimate themselves in terms of silence and the possibility to get to know yourself."

"So, it's about getting to know your inner self?"

"Yes, that is where our strength lies, and that is what demons find hard to break down. It's like that thyme plant." He pointed to his prized thyme plant on a raised box planter. "To many, people see it only as a weed at first glance. But, if you pause a little longer, different shades of green appear. And if you get close, touch it, smell its fragrance, the life of the organism reveals itself. The details come into focus." He plucked a thyme plant and held it to Clarisse's nose.

She closed her eyes, taking a deep breath and absorbing the unique scent.

"Some of the oldest advice throughout history is to get to know yourself, and I think any advice that has lasted for more than a thousand years is worth considering."

"Your silence helps you understand who you are?"

"Yes. You should try it. It's tempting to think of silence as simply the absence of noise, something that's empty and amounts to nothing. The opposite is true. Silence is something. It's rich, a quality. I believe it's exclusive and luxurious and is a key to unlocking new ways of thinking."

Clarisse nodded, wanting to listen to his wisdom all day long.

"It helps me connect with my God when I meditate and pray, to be closer to Him. Demons cannot penetrate that silence. They have no concept of it, as they live in a world of noise, distraction, temptation, lust, and the need to conquer souls."

"Practicing silence takes a while, and it can't happen straight away, so discipline?" she asked.

"Silence is very much about being in the present. It's about getting to know yourself better. Sometimes that can be uncomfortable and disturbing. And yes, time-consuming because you have to disassociate yourself with your current lifestyle for a while—work, school, money, career, ambition … you know, the list goes on."

She continued listening as it was not often that Shamy would provide insights into his ways.

"So, this is what I reckon in a nutshell … If you can think about silence as a strength, when we perform our spiritual rites, like the flashbacks, you can see things that others would miss. You're in tune with your environment then."

After a short walk around the herb garden, Shamy asked her if she was ready to take on a risky spiritual meditation. He called it a *droplet in thyme.* It was an ancient potion made of holy oil mixed with a variety of rare herbs in a thyme ointment, sanctified by a line of shamans extending over hundreds of years. A droplet of this ointment was enough to continue the handover from shaman to shaman without breaking the power and sanctity of the potion. It was a rarely used technique often fraught with dangerous consequences if one was not spiritually strong enough.

"Am I ready for something like that?" asked Clarisse, doubting her ability to take on such a task that was left for the most experienced shaman.

"Yes, you have a strong will. But there are some rules. First, you cannot interfere with the vision or make yourself known to the demon, no matter how painful it becomes."

"I can only watch it?"

"Yes, it's not a flashback. We are visioning the future, and that's something we can't mess around with."

"What do I do when I'm in the vision?"

"Observe, watch every bit of detail. The demon leaves a trail of clues, his evil signature." Shamy plucked thyme from his garden and held it to his nose. "Perfect. This will do."

"Why do you use thyme in your spirituality?"

"Thyme has psychic qualities, luv. My ancestors understood this well. Europeans would place it in coffins to help the dead pass on to the next world. It grants courage to warriors of the faith."

Shamy led the way back to the shed and got straight to work. He opened the old mortise lock to a unique, ornate storage cabinet made of thick iron and decorated with religious motifs. Then he took out the sacred ointment containing the thyme extract that was in a small, round metal jar the size of his palm. He reached for the incense burner next and placed the freshly picked thyme inside it while adding burning incense. It was time to light it.

"Come over here. I need to place the ointment on the palms of your hands and forehead," said Shamy.

The essence of thyme started to fill the room, a relaxed, soft smell that infiltrated her nostrils. It was sublime, and she had never felt so calm.

Shamy took hold of her hands, rubbing the ointment on her palms and forehead in the sign of the cross. He then held both of her hands with the tips of his fingers, closed his eyes, and prayed an ancient Byzantine devotion to God.

Clarisse felt her mind sway as she closed her eyes then reawakened in a different time and place. She was standing at Old Tailem Church, next to a window overlooking the graveyard. People were everywhere, and the ghost town had turned into a theme park. It was opening day in full swing.

Next to the graveyard, she could see children running in a children's play area. The jumping castles and slides proved popular as the children jumped around emphatically, bouncing off each other in synchronized motion.

There was a magician and performers who juggled balls into the air and threw about a hula hoop. Another performer completed perfectly executed somersaults. Near the shrub, a puppeteer had set up a display, and a ventriloquist held a dummy, preparing. His assistants called the kids over to sit in the picnic chairs laid out in front of the ventriloquist. The dummy called out in a squeaky voice to encourage the kids to come over and watch the performance. It worked, as children noticed, charmed by the boyish, high-pitched rendition.

A puppet is talking to us, they thought.

As the kids gathered around the ventriloquist and took their seats, the dummy made all sorts of funny voices, and they laughed.

"Does anyone want to see what I have behind this curtain?" asked the dummy. "Come on; who wants to go first?"

Two boys put their hands up immediately. One boy had a small symbol on his forehead—a hexagon imprint—while the other did not. The dummy called over the boy with the imprint, and then the assistant chaperoned him behind the white curtain. The hexagonal sign meant the demon had targeted them.

"Come on; it's a nice surprise. You will like it," the dummy encouraged him.

The boy walked reluctantly toward the curtain, led by the assistant holding his hand. He was shy and looked back a few times as the other kids forced him on with banter. When he was next to the curtain, a white-gloved hand pulled him behind until there was no sight of the boy, only his gray shadow reflected by the sun from behind the white curtain.

"Abracadabra." The dummy pulled out his wand. "Watch him disappear with the touch of my wand."

The children all gasped in amazement as the boy's shadow disappeared.

The assistant turned toward Clarisse, red eyes radiating fiercely, and her face screwed up. She was one of the evil crew who had shifted her image to draw in the child.

Clarisse sensed the danger but could not do anything, bound by the rules provided by Shamy.

The dummy tried to change their focus by directing the children away from the curtain with its subjective humor. Meanwhile, the boy was being dragged into the shrub by the demon with the white hand. Another child being kidnapped. The devil no longer had the Raggedy Ann doll to draw the children in and had become inventive.

The boy kicked and screamed, but nobody could hear him, drowned out by the playground noise and music pumping from the jumping castle. He scraped his fingers along the soil, frantically grabbing hold of anything he could, his puppy dog eyes in shock as tears rolled down his face. The strain to free himself showed on his pushed-out cheeks and screwed-up forehead, forced upon by intense fear.

Clarisse wanted to help him. It hurt her immensely, and she tried to break loose of the rules, to run for him, but she couldn't. She was caught in an exhibition of torment and frustration.

The boy managed to hold onto a low-lying branch with both hands, gripping on for his life. He anchored his legs around another log. The tug of war slowed the demon down.

He kept on screaming, "Mummy, Daddy ... help, help!"

Clarisse's heart pounding, hands sweating, she grimaced and ground her teeth, wrestling and jostling to reach for him. Still, there was nothing she could do.

The clues ... Look for clues, she thought.

Clarisse quickly glanced across the playground, looking for similarities and signs that appeared out of the ordinary. She had a mystical knack for spotting things that could go unnoticed.

The juggler pranced around like a joker and had managed to clasp on to the interest of a girl. The girl was mesmerized, in a trancelike state, drawn to the juggler, who spun her colorful balls into the air in a coordinated motion. The girl also had a hexagonal imprint on her forehead.

Clarisse scoured the rest of the playground to see if other children carried the same imprint, but there were none.

The child stepped closer to the juggler. The balls flipped and bounced in the air with intensity, faster, higher, and counterclockwise. The girl was caught in the motion of the balls, unknowingly following the juggler slowly toward the shrub. With each step, the child was attached to the juggler like a magnet. It was another kidnapping in the making.

A horrible, ominous face flashed in front of her, nose to nose. Ghoulish, white skin and shrewd, red eyes glowed like a vibrant fire. A chin that twirled upward, wolf fangs pegged like horse teeth penetrating in front of skinny outstretched lips, a purple tongue hissing, slithering in and out of its mouth. Underneath its eyes, the darkest of circles bagged down its cheeks.

Clarisse shrieked. It was the most devilish portrayal she had ever seen. It was the face of a demon, possibly the master. Who else had the potency to see through the ritualistic vision? Was this what Shamy had meant when he had said priests returned mentally insane after experiencing an encounter with a powerful demon master?

Clarisse felt a tug behind her and turned around to

find Shamy clasping her hand. He had sensed the danger and wanted to pull her out to safety.

She grabbed his arm and nodded, signaling it was time for her to leave, and quickly. But something else caught her from the other side. A cold, bony sensation and the piercing touch of long nails started pricking into her skin. The demon had taken hold of her and was not letting go.

It was a struggle between the two protagonists—evil and good. Shamy had to act fast, as he was losing his hold on her.

In a desperate attempt to save Clarisse from the clutches of the evil master, he held up the *carbonados* in his right hand, punching it into the air with a fist. It was the sign of defiance, creating enough energy to push back the demon with a pulsating force.

Clarisse was released from the tinderbox of evil as the shaman broke the juncture between them.

Disconnected from the vision, they returned to the shed. Clarisse was sapped of her mental stamina, having endured a horrifying event.

Shamy had warned her of the fragility of the task and the possible interjection of the demon master, an example of what lengths the evil force would go to stop witnesses.

It had been a close call, and only the experience of Shamy and his knowledge had saved Clarisse.

It was time for a debrief.

Shamy waited for Clarisse to settle down, still rattled by the visions. Watching children scream and being taken away from their parents by an evil force represented her worst fears. Nobody in their right mind would want to endure such a heinous crime.

Shamy made a new pot of tea, and the fragrance helped calm Clarisse. He poured her a cup without asking, knowing she needed something to help her relax. The thyme essence still lingered in the room, and that helped soothe her senses, also.

"When you are ready, luv, we need to debrief on what you saw. I know it was a harrowing experience, but I need you to try hard and recollect any clues," said Shamy.

Clarisse nodded without saying a word and sipped on her tea. Holding the cup with both hands for security, she needed to latch on to something soothing and warm.

"I saw a hexagonal imprint on both children dragged away, but not the others," she said.

Shamy pulled out his ancient leather book with the embossed image and flicked over the pages. "Did it look like this?"

"Yes, yes, that's it."

"It's the mark of the devil, the imprint they use to identify souls."

"They know who they are going to take?"

"They can't take all the children. Not enough resources, and it would foil their plan, bring it into the open." Shamy flicked over the next page. "They like to work by stealth."

"How does the demon choose a child? There were so many of them in the playground."

"Our resident demon didn't select them. His master did."

"So, they can't kidnap all the children?"

"No, only those marked by the hexagonal imprint." Shamy closed his book and gazed toward Clarisse, looking serious. "Now I need you to think hard. Was there anything else you saw?"

Clarisse put her cup down and looked ahead toward the altar. She pondered and thought intensely.

"Well, hold on … yes, I did."

Shamy was anxious for her response, fidgeting with his rosary.

"I saw Kezza standing in the middle of the play area, looking straight ahead. She didn't attempt to save the boy, even though she could see what was happening before her own eyes." Clarisse turned toward Shamy, making eye contact. "Is she one of them?"

"I would call her a sympathizer rather than a demon," said Shamy. He got up from his chair to stretch his back. "There are always sympathizers in the mortal sense that help the demons achieve their aim, a sort of crossover support. In return, they are rewarded with privileges."

"They've made a pact?"

"Let's call it a deal that works both ways."

There was a sudden knock on the shed door.

"It's me, mate. What are you doing in there, having a conference?" Digger laughed.

Shamy peered outside the window and found Digger's crimson FJ Holden parked nearby. "Digger's come to pick you up."

He escorted Clarisse to the door then whispered, "We need a plan for opening day. It's only two days away now. How 'bout tomorrow, luv?"

She nodded with a small smile, thinking, *Do I need to go through this again?*

"Do you remember the faces of the two children?" asked Shamy.

Clarisse stopped and gazed at him, a teardrop forming in the corner of her eye. "How can I ever forget what I saw? Yes, of course, like a photo."

The drive back to the motel felt longer than usual. Clarisse was apprehensive, with a lot on her mind. Digger sensed her worries and tried some banter to cheer her up.

"It's a ripper of a day today, luv. Blue skies, no wind, and not too hot. Might put on a barbie this afternoon if the weather holds up."

Clarisse was daydreaming and did not respond.

"Are you all right? Did the shaman charm you with his wisdom again, huh?"

She rolled down her window to let in the distinctive smell of the bush. She inhaled a deep breath and sucked up the eucalyptus fragrance. "I have always liked the smell of the bush, and the clean air. It clears the mind."

"Yeah, you're from the big smoke, so I don't appreciate it as much as you. I suppose you get used to it after a while." Digger rolled down his window, too, and stuck his head out. "I can smell it. It's stronger on this part of the road."

"I'm worried about opening day," admitted Clarisse abruptly.

"Ah, she'll be right, luv. I've got everything organized. I'm in charge of security for the day, remember?" He had a cocky smile, and his face exuded confidence. "I have the ghost hunters ready to go with their equipment, and these guys are hardcore. They know their shit." Digger laughed. "They are coming tomorrow to set up. You can meet them if you like."

Clarisse turned and gazed at Digger. "Your security staff can't see demons."

"Is that what you and Shamy have been talking about?"

"We believe something wrong is going to happen if we don't have a plan." Clarisse took another deep breath as she glanced out the window and sighed.

"Knowing Shamy the way I do, I reckon he has ideas." Digger grabbed his bottle of water and gulped it down. He was thirsty from the drive to Shamy's place, and his car still had no air conditioning. He flashed his eyes across to Clarisse while trying to negotiate a winding bend. "But I think you guys did more than talk spiritual stuff, and I reckon Shamy is onto something."

Clarisse did not mutter a word, expressionless and cautious about what to say.

"I have known him for thirty years, luv, so I sort of know what he does. He is the town's shaman, after all."

"He wants to discuss a plan tomorrow. Can you make it?"

"She'll be right, luv. After I sort out the ghost hunters, I will pick you up. Around midday?"

Clarisse nodded. She had all the time in the world and no other plans.

"And why don't you and Harry join me for the barbie this arvo? I'll have heaps of snags and cold ones."

"You mean beer?" Clarisse smiled. She loved Digger's Aussie accent. "I'm sure Harry will love to come along and talk about his project all night."

Digger laughed. "I'm sure I can handle it."

12 THE SILENT ENERGY

"Over here, luv. I want ya to meet the ghost hunters I spoke to you about. Meet Jason and Mike. They run a company called Spiritual Encounters," said Digger.

Clarisse nodded and welcomed them to Old Tailem Town. "I like your business name. I see you have lots of equipment in the back of the ute."

They were two weird-looking guys—long hair tied in a ponytail, wearing fitted, custom-made tracksuits with their company logo embroidered on the jacket.

"Oh yeah, we got the latest detection devices in infrared imaging and sound recording," said Jason. He took a step forward, attracted by Clarisse's presence, and wouldn't stop smiling. "Digger's going to show us where to set up. He reckons the graveyard next to the church."

"I would look at the perimeter where the unmarked graves are nearer to the shrubs. We've had a couple of close encounters there," Clarisse explained.

"Seems like you know your stuff," said Jason. He took another step closer to Clarisse. "He mentioned you have a spiritual connection with the dead."

Clarisse looked at Digger with inquiring eyes.

"Okay, time to go, you lot," said Digger, looking away from Clarisse in embarrassment.

When they were all ready to go, Digger called out to Clarisse and said, "I will pick you up in an hour, and we can head off to the shaman."

Clarisse waved and gave him a thumbs-up in acknowledgement. It was enough time for her and Harry to have a bite to eat.

The midday sun had a sting to it, but it felt fine under Shamy's veranda that was filtered by crawling vines that had luscious white flowers in bloom. Shamy had anticipated the hot day and had provided ice-cold tea for everyone.

One thing Clarisse liked about Shamy was his hospitality. Even though he was regarded as a hermit and a grumpy individual by the townsfolk, once he got to know you, he always showed his country-style warmth.

Harry had decided to join them for the meeting. His communication project complete meant he had lots of free time on his hands.

Shamy poured the cold iced tea for everyone then pulled out his ancient book, shuffling through it until he found the page he wanted.

"So, let me begin. Tomorrow is opening day, and I am certain the demon will attempt to kidnap children. I believe it will happen in the graveyard, near the unmarked graves," said Shamy.

"I found out Kezza planned a kids' entertainment in the vacant lot next to the graveyard —jumping castles, a magician, and jugglers. I also learned there will be a puppet show." Digger pulled out the planned activities flyer that he had found at the motel and put it on the table in front of them. He shook his head. "Ya know, I've never trusted that woman. She's sly as a fox."

"How about your ghost hunters? Are they in town?" Shamy took a sip of tea then wiped his mouth with his hand, dropping some onto his pants as he laid his cup on the table.

"Yeah, those guys are weird city folk, but they know their shit. And you should see the equipment—hi-tech stuff." Digger appeared excited, like a kid with a new toy. He was thinking about how he could incorporate the ghost hunters into his paranormal tours. "They're putting their monitors inside the church and the infrared cameras and sound devices around the graveyard perimeter, near the unmarked graves and shrubs. We will be able to see the bastards coming."

Harry, typically the quiet one, intervened by saying, "What about at the rocks where they tried to take little Oliver? Can we put an infrared camera there? It's their staging site, right?"

Digger patted Harry on the back. "Good on ya, mate. I didn't think about that. It's a brilliant idea!"

Shamy offered a rare smile and opened his book. "This is the symbol I saw in my vision, and Clarisse supports it. It's the hexagonal sign of the demon. It belongs to a branch of powerful demons whose plan is to take over small towns, sleepy hallows, and expand their reach."

He pointed to the intricate marks on the hexagonal design. "The marks of the hexagon verifies the symbol belongs to the demons. It has been around since my ancestors. Shamans better than I fought battles to reclaim towns in the name of God. Some of them left wounded and scarred from their intervention."

Shamy turned another page then pointed to another image. "This is the master demon that controls the hexagonal sign and oversees the rank and file."

"The master has a master?" asked Clarisse.

"Yes, he has lieutenants to organize his work."

"You talk about it as though they are an army," said Digger.

"The order that I belong to was formed to fight organized advances by demons. We had to group up, train, and become recluse to keep our spirits clean to counter their relentless attacks. We have been fighting this battle for centuries. We are called the Order of the Sepaline, but it's not something I want to advertise to the townsfolk, got it?"

Everyone was quiet as they absorbed the shaman's history lesson. The evil was more ingrained than they had realized.

"So, what's our plan?" asked Harry. For a skeptic, he was keen on stopping the demon in its tracks.

They all looked at each other, waiting for a lead. Harry was right; without a proper plan on opening day, how were they going to catch the demon red-handed?

"You're a communications expert, Harry, right? So, why don't you and I take the ghost hunters to the rocks and set up some equipment there? You know, set up a warning system?" said Digger.

"Sure, I can do that. At least we will know when they are coming. It will give us time to act."

Shamy went back to the page with the hexagonal drawing and turned it toward Clarisse. "Remember this picture, luv. You and I are going to keep a lookout for any children with the hexagonal sign. And what about your memory of the kids?"

"I can't forget their faces. I will know straight away. But something is missing, Shamy …"

He was silent for a moment as he looked around the table with a defiant stare. "You want to know how I will stop the evil?"

Everyone nodded, not uttering a word.

"You leave that bit to me. And trust me; I have a plan of action." Shamy had a scheme laid out, but he did not want to sidetrack anyone from their focus on opening day. He took a sip of his tea then set his cup on the table. "I only ask one thing. When you spot the children in danger, relocate them to the church as soon as you can. They will be safe there, I assure you."

Shamy and Clarisse stared at each other, knowing perfectly well the significance of tomorrow. The demon no longer had the Raggedy Ann doll and had had to become creative.

13 OPENING DAY

Old Tailem Town was abuzz with people preparing for the big event. Opening day had finally arrived.

For the first time in nearly one hundred years, the pioneering village would be awash with people, ready to shed its ghost town tag, at least for today. The motel was full of patrons from the media, facilities, and entertainment organizers, something it had not experienced before. It had managed to scrape through on passersby and people off the beaten track, but today was payday for Kezza and her financiers. She was in an uncharacteristic jovial mood. And although she was aware of the dangers that lurked within the town, she didn't care since the profit made way for the welfare and safety of others.

Despite all the facilities up and running in the pioneering village, which included the old ironworks, the traditional western-style bank, and pioneering food stalls,

Digger's paranormal tours were the main feature for the day, running every hour from nine a.m. to five p.m. The whole town and the success of the pioneering village evolved around his paranormal tours, and the media loved it.

Digger had constant requests from local radio and television shows for interviews and private tours. Within the space of twenty-four hours, he had become a celebrity. His outgoing, ocker personality played right into the hands of the media entourage who were at pains to show the genuineness of this rural outpost.

Harry, for his part, was busy helping set up the ghostbusting equipment. He successfully connected a link over the rocks where the demon had kidnapped little Oliver. Harry commented on how the equipment was state of the art. If there was to be any paranormal movement at the rocks or around the cemetery perimeter, it would show up immediately on the monitors.

Although Harry was a skeptic and liked to prove the paranormal stuff was all fake, his time in Hartley had softened his point of view. He had seen reliable evidence that unexplained phenomena existed. He could not provide a logical explanation for the events and, as far as he was concerned, they remained unsolvable.

For Harry, being with the ghost hunters offered

another opportunity to delve further into his technical assessment of the spirit world. He was starting to like it and thought about setting up his own ghostbusting equipment one day.

The surveillance equipment was in the back room of the church, next to the vestry, which was the size of a small office yet was enough room to fit three LCD monitors. Any sign of movement by spirits would appear on the monitors as infrared. This equipment was precise and used the energy source, a marker, that spirits carried with them, to pick up their presence.

Before such equipment was around, ghost hunters were usually spirit mediums or telepaths with powers to connect to the spirit world, which was often a personal and risky activity. Mediumship was the practice of mediating communication between spirits of the dead and living human beings. The ghostbusting technology used today had made such mediums redundant.

Shamy remained in the safety of the church, away from the commotion of visitors.

To allow coordination and avoid overcrowding, each busload of children would span a two-hour tour before a new group arrived. This meant Clarisse had to inspect the playground every two hours, looking for the hexagonal signs. So, even though they were expecting a lot of downtime, they had to act quickly when the demon struck. The whole team—Harry, Digger, the ghostbusters, and Clarisse—had to be ready to intervene at the right moment to stop the kidnappings.

Digger was keeping an eye on Kezza throughout the day. A suspected demon sympathizer, they were concerned she had planned the events to ensure the demon and his evil crew could pounce. The demon needed things he could not control—children and entertainers to draw them in. And most importantly, a ventriloquist located close to the shrubs next to the playground. Her role was to have all those logistics in place. If Kezza was prancing around the playground, it was a sign that a kidnapping was imminent.

The afternoon sun was glaring as folks crowded the attraction when Harry contacted Clarisse on her cell phone with a sense of urgency in his voice. "We have a paranormal detection at the rocks, moving steadily toward the playground—three blips."

"Looks like we're on," responded Clarisse. "I will let Digger know. He's only ten yards away. Oh, and what do they look like on the monitor?"

"This equipment is amazing! I can see the outline of …" Harry paused. "Yeah, the outline of demon-like figures."

Clarisse scoured the play area near the ventriloquist, who was preparing to start his show. Then came her first detection of the hexagonal sign. The imprint was on a boy, not more than eight years old. He took a seat with other children at the ventriloquist stage and laughed as the ventriloquist dummy made funny voices at the children, trying to grab their attention.

Across from the ventriloquist, where entertainers juggled balls and hula hoops, another child, a girl of the same age, carried the hexagonal sign.

Digger called back on his cell phone and pointed at Kezza, who was walking around with her arms crossed, looking like she was on a mission.

"We need to get the girl directly in front of you to the church. Mousey hair, tied in a bun, wearing jeans and a red tracksuit jacket," said Clarisse.

"Okay, got it," responded Digger. He nodded and gave her a visual thumbs-up.

She was not sure how a stranger like Digger was going to get a child to change her focus from an entertainer to the church, but that was the strength of the man. People loved and trusted him on first impression. So, if anyone could do it, it was him.

Clarisse received another call from Harry. "They are

on the edges of the shrub, directly in front of you. They look heinous. Be careful."

She turned toward the church and waved confidently at Harry as he watched on from the church window.

Within a couple of seconds, the boy was at the ventriloquist's stage, talking to the dummy and laughing loudly. He was then led to the back of the curtain by the dummy as it played on the boy's curiosity. A perfect trap.

It was difficult witnessing the ventriloquist carry out the kidnapping, an accessory to a crime.

The boy remained behind the stage curtain for a long time while the ventriloquist commenced his show to divert everyone's attention.

Clarisse quickly turned her head and noticed Digger walking the girl and her mother to the safety of the church with a bag of prizes and a large lollipop in hand, entertained by his humor.

Thank God she is safe, thought Clarisse.

Harry called Clarisse again and said, "One click away and right in front of you, next to the boy. You need to do something now. I'm coming out." He ended the call and rushed toward Clarisse, nearly tripping down the front steps of the church.

The sounds of children playing drowned the screams of the boy. The demon had latched on to his arms, dragging him into the shrub.

Clarisse was close enough to hear the screams and dashed toward the boy with Harry in pursuit.

"Mummy, Daddy … help, help!" The boy was breathing irregularly, in the midst of a panic attack. He kicked and shook his body, fighting with every bit of strength he could muster before releasing a loud, piercing cry of fear. The high-pitched squeal filtered through Clarisse and gave her the shivers, but she had to stay calm and focused for the boy's sake.

Harry rushed past her and dived for the boy's legs with both hands gripping firmly, chest side down and his face above the ground, spitting out dried leaves and dirt.

The demons did not make themselves visible to mortals, and even Digger could not spot them. Somehow, though, Harry had been able to connect with the spirit world and maintain a clear image.

Clarisse followed suit, grabbing on to the boy's jeans. It was a tug of war, but they were losing their grip on him. The demon was powerful, and he had the assistance of his evil crew.

The whole rescue was being caught on camera as the ghost hunters watched on in the infrared images of three demons clamped on to the boy. Even though experienced ghost hunters, they had never seen anything this coordinated. These demons worked like a coordinated pack, efficiently timed, with the element of surprise.

Shamy was in the crypt, calling on the spiritual powers vested in him by the ancient Order of the Sepaline. The timing and circumstances had to be aligned.

He opened the black box and took out the black *carbonados*, laying it on the altar in an ornate metallic object the size of a jewelry box. Next to it was a Byzantine cross and an incense burner that had started uplifting the frankincense.

He opened his ancient book and turned to the same page with the hexagonal diagram and a paragraph of prayer. It was written in a different language—old Byzantine. He had learned to read it from his father.

Shamy lifted his hands in the air as he continued praying and clapped his hands three times. A pulse of energy radiated outward. It did not hurt anyone and felt like a vibration. It was the energy of silence, and it pounded the demons like a ten-story building, excruciating and piercing their spirits with one hundred daggers. The energy of silence was so intense that the demons covered their ears as they scrambled and rolled on the ground. It was slowly destroying them. They had no option but to flee back to the underworld while still in one piece or face turning into stardust.

The demon and his crew turned toward the ground, wobbled, and made heinous sounds. Their hands and feet clawed up, and they were immobilized. Their blood-stained faces melted in the midday sun as their metaphysical bodies turned red and caught fire. Flickers of light swirled upward like a tornado, and then, in the shape of a dagger, pierced downward in one mighty swoop through the ground to the underworld. They were no more in the mortal realm.

The demon and the evil crew were defeated. Old Tailem Town was no longer the stronghold of evil.

Clarisse was inside the church now, watching over the two children who had been saved from the grips of the attempted kidnappings. The two children were oblivious of the danger they had faced, and due to Clarisse's quick thinking, they would grow up to live an everyday life.

The demon had lost his powers and those souls that had strong bonds to the mortal world had been released from their captivity, free to move on to the afterlife.

Digger stood next to an unmarked grave with his arms crossed, waiting for something to happen. No one had told him to go there; he had simply felt an urge to be in this part of the graveyard.

An apparition, transparent but visible, appeared. It was his niece, sitting on the unmarked grave with her legs crossed. She smiled at him and held her hands out, wanting to hold her uncle and hug him.

He stood there, watery-eyed and with a solemn look. It had been fifteen years since he had lost her to the evil force, yet there she was, as beautiful as ever, wearing the same clothes as that fateful day and her pitch-black hair tied in a ponytail. It was precisely the way she had looked when she had been taken by the demon that horrible evening.

How could he forget the horror he had gone through after losing her? Not a single day passed without thinking about her. He blamed himself for what had happened, like an unrelenting curse.

She stood up with her arms reaching outward, encouraging him to come forward. And he walked up to her and held her tightly as a tear slid down the side of his face. It was a magical touch, a small moment in time that lasted an eternity.

"It wasn't your fault, Uncle," she whispered. "But I am leaving now." She put her head on his chest. "I will be fine ... Don't worry about me anymore."

Digger didn't want to let go as he brushed his hands over her head in a caressing motion.

She let go of him and waved goodbye for the last time. She was going to a better place, and he knew it. Leaving behind the shackles of the demon and his evil crew, her soul transitioned to the afterlife.

Digger waved goodbye and blew her a kiss as he stood stoic and brave. It was the second time he had to see her go, but this time under different circumstances. He was at peace with himself now.

Clarisse watched on from the church garden. Although regular people could not see Digger's niece—looking as though he was hugging fresh air—Clarisse could see her in full view.

Clarisse turned away when she felt someone tugging at her from behind—Little Charlie's apparition.

He was chirpier and smiling without holding on to a rope. Cleaned up like a sweet child, he looked prim and proper. The long socks, knee-length shorts, and white tailored shirt fit perfectly. His hair was cut short, swept back and to the side. He tilted his head with a puppy dog look and gazed at her unrelentingly. He was so cute that all Clarisse wanted to do was caress him and take him home. But it was wishful thinking. Little Charlie had been released from the shadows of evil and was ready to transition to a better place in the spirit world.

Clarisse gave him one big hug and kissed his cheek, knowing it was his time. She was sad and teary but also happy to see him move on. She had saved him through her perseverance, knowing that transient souls could be freed from the cusp of darkness, if your belief was strong enough.

He waved goodbye with a radiant smile, his apparition slowly becoming translucent until he was gone.

The demon had suffered a significant loss. His master was unforgiving. There were no second chances in the underworld. Punished and sent to the confines of darkness, fire, and brimstone, it was a harsh punishment. The demon master had shut down his affiliate and no longer sought to take over Old Tailem Town. It was like closing a chapter within a larger organization. But that didn't mean Clarisse was off the hook. Demon masters had long memories, and it would pursue her to the next staging point. Revenge was on the list.

Clarisse made her way to the crypt at a brisk pace to see Shamy, dodging all the tourists who were unaware of what had taken place. Once inside the church, there was a serene feeling, a sense of quiet and peace. It felt like a church again.

She lifted the trapdoor and made her way down the stairs. The air was filled with incense, and Shamy sat on an ornate metal chair next to the altar, resting with his arms on his thighs and his hands over his face. She was not sure if he was praying.

Shamy heard her presence, looked up, and smiled.

There was the solitary chair in the crypt, so Clarisse sat on the staircase snug between two steps.

"You never explained to me about the Order of the Sepaline. Just snippets here and there." She felt now was a good time to learn more about the shaman's ancestry.

He looked at her, nodded, and then crossed his arms. "It was around 950 AD, Constantine VII was the Byzantine Emperor. The Order of the Sepaline was a protectorate of Christ, defending mankind against evil forces—demons." He took a deep breath. "There were two monks, Arsenios and Kostas, and they were the leaders of the order at the time.

"It was during a meeting of the monks in the Church of the Holy Sepulchre in Jerusalem that they confronted a legion of demons. What unfolded was an immense battle with the underworld. Many monks died in the confrontation, but the evil was subdued for centuries in the power of ... the *carbonados*."

Clarisse listened with intent, fascinated by the story.

She adjusted her seating on the uncomfortable steps but was happy to weather the stress on her bones to hear his story.

"Constantine was not happy with the Order of the Sepaline—too much spiritual power. He felt threatened. So, he sent his troops to arrest the monks and disband the order. He wanted no remnants left anywhere.

"Through the centuries we expanded to all parts of the world, working under secrecy."

"That explains why you keep to yourself, like a secret society?"

"Yes, because we can't talk about our history and bloodline to anyone."

"So, why are you telling me?"

"I'm taking a risk, I suppose. But there is something about you I trust. I know you won't tell anyone, not even your Harry."

Clarisse promised to keep their discussion a secret, like a bond.

Harry accepted a communication project assignment in the state of Victoria, in the rural ghost town of Walhalla. Once a flourishing gold mining town, established in 1862, it had become a ghost town with few residents.

Clarisse and Harry packed their belongings, ready to leave Old Tailem Town. They were not going to miss the motel and its lousy food and were looking forward to their next move.

Kezza watched from a distance, starry-eyed, making sure they were finally on their way.

Digger helped load their bags into Harry's ute. He was the ever-optimistic type as he gave his thumbs-up and blinked, underpinned by a broad smile. Shamy preferred to wave and nod in a low-key manner as they drove off down the main street. Clarisse had promised to keep in touch with Shamy. There was so much more she wanted to learn from him. She already considered him her spiritual advisor.

"Do you like the gift from Shamy?" asked Clarisse. It was a smaller version of the *carbonados*, a black, sparkling, round stone. "He said it would keep us safe."

"It sparkles like a diamond," Harry said, glancing at Clarisse before returning his eyes to the road. "I have been thinking of buying the ghostbusting equipment. Maybe we can be a tag team?"

Clarisse smiled. "A team of spirit hunters? Hm … I like that idea."

As Harry turned onto the main road, they heard a rattle in the back of the ute.

"Did you hear that, Harry?"

"Yeah, it's a weird scraping sound coming from inside a box. Must be something loose."

Clarisse nodded in acknowledgement, though the sound was familiar.

She glanced toward Harry and said, "Did you hear the scraping again?"

With one hand on the wheel and the other resting on the driver's side window, he shrugged. "I can't see anything in the rearview mirror. I'll check when we stop for gas."

The end

ABOUT THE AUTHOR

Janice is an emerging Australian author who lives with her family in Melbourne. Her recent publication, *Haunting in Hartley*, reached number one on the Amazon kindle ranking for Occult, Supernatural, and Ghosts and Haunted Houses categories, for hot new releases and bestsellers.

Janice is a finalist in the Readers' Favorite 2020 International Book Awards in fiction-supernatural and was awarded the distinguished favorite prize for paranormal horror at the New York City Big Book Awards 2020.

Janice is well-versed in her cultural superstitions and how they influence daily life and customs. She has developed a passion and style for writing ghost and supernatural novels for new adult readers.

Her books contain heart-thumping, bone-chilling, and thought-provoking ghost and paranormal experiences that deliver a new twist to every tale.

www.janicetremayne.com.au

author@janicetremayne.com

www.ingramcontent.com/pod-product-compliance
Lightning Source LLC
Chambersburg PA
CBHW050155120726
47903CB00002B/627